PENGUIN BOOKS

NEWS FROM THRUSH GREEN

Although 'Miss Read' wishes to remain anonymous, she says that she is a teacher by profession who started writing after the Second World War, beginning with light essays written under her own name, mainly for *Punch*. She writes on educational and country matters for various journals, and also works as a scriptwriter for the B.B.C.

Her hobbies are theatre-going, listening to music, and reading. She is married, with one daughter, and lives in a Berkshire village.

'Miss Read' has published many books, including *Village School* (1955), *Village Diary* (1957), *Storm in the Village* (1958), *Thrush Green* (1959), *Fresh from the Country* (1960), *Winter in Thrush Green* (1961), *Miss Clare Remembers* (1962), an anthology, *Country Bunch* (1963), *Over the Gate* (1964), *The Market Square* (1966), *Village Christmas* (1966), *The Howards of Caxley* (1967), *The Fairacre Festival* (1968), two books for children, *Hobby Horse Cottage* and *Hob and the Horse-bat,* and The Red Bus Series for the very young. Her latest book is *Tyler's Row* (1972).

MISS READ

News from Thrush Green

PENGUIN BOOKS

Penguin Books Ltd, Harmondsworth, Middlesex, England
Penguin Books Australia Ltd, Ringwood, Victoria, Australia
Penguin Books Canada Ltd, 41 Steelcase Road West, Markham, Ontario, Canada
Penguin Books (N.Z.) Ltd, 182–190 Wairau Road, Auckland 10, New Zealand

—

First published by Michael Joseph 1970
Published in Penguin Books 1973
Reprinted 1975

—

Copyright © 'Miss Read', 1970

—

Made and printed in Great Britain by
Cox & Wyman Ltd, London, Reading and Fakenham
Set in Monotype Garamond

FOR

MARJORIE AND GLEN

WITH LOVE

'You are now collecting your People delightfully, getting them exactly into such a spot as is the delight of my life; 3 or 4 Families in a Country Village is the very thing to work on.'

JANE AUSTEN *in a letter written to her niece Anna who was then writing novels*

Contents

1. *For Sale – Tullivers*

IF you live at Thrush Green you can expect your morning post between 7.30 and 8.15 a.m.

If it is Willie Bond's week to deliver the letters, then they will be early. But if Willie Marchant is the postman then it is no use fretting and fuming. The post will arrive well after eight o'clock, and you may as well resign yourself to the fact.

'It just shows you can't go by looks,' Thrush Green residents tell each other frequently. Willie Bond weighs fifteen stone, is short-legged and short-necked, and puffs in a truly alarming fashion as he pushes his bicycle up the steep hill from the post office at Lulling. His eyes are mere slits in the pink and white moon of his chubby face, and his nickname of Porky is still used by those who were his schoolfellows.

Willie Marchant, on the other hand, is a gaunt bean-pole of a fellow with a morose, lined face, and a cigarette stub in the corner of his mouth. He scorns to dismount at Thrush Green's sharp hill, but tacks purposefully back and forth across the road with a fine disregard for the motorists who suffer severe shock when coming upon him suddenly at his manoeuvres. He was once knocked off his bicycle as he made a sharp right-hand turn from one bank to the other, but escaped with a grazed knee and a torn trouser leg.

Dr Bailey, whose house was nearby, had treated both postman and driver, and found that the motorist, though unscarred, was by far the more severely shaken of the two. But despite this mishap, the violent remarks of later motorists and the advice given unstintingly by his clients on Thrush Green, Willie continues to proceed on his erratic course every other week.

The fact that both men have the same Christian name might, at first sight, seem confusing, but there are distinct advantages. As Ella Bembridge remarked once at a Thrush Green cocktail party, in a booming voice heard by all present:

'It's jolly useful when you're upstairs coping with your bust bodice or bloomers, and you hear whoever-it-is plonking down the letters on the hall table! I just shout down: "Thanks, Willie", and you know you'll be all right.'

There had been a sudden burst of animated conversation as Ella's fellow-guests, embarrassed or simply amused by Ella's unguarded remarks, sought to tell each other hastily of their own arrangements for receiving and disposing of their mail.

'I have had to install one of those wire cage things,' said Harold Shoosmith, the bachelor who lives in one of the handsomest houses on the green. 'Since the puppy came, nothing's safe on the floor. He ate a cheque for six pounds ten, and the rates' demand, all in one gulp last Thursday. I didn't mind the latter, naturally, but I hated to see the cheque going down.'

'We leave our letters sticking out of the flap,' said the rector, 'and Willie takes them!'

'Not if it's a north wind,' his wife Dimity reminded him. 'The rain blows in and drenches them. He has to open the door then, and take them from the window-sill.'

Winnie Bailey, the doctor's wife, said she tried to put hers in the post-box on the corner of the green. It made her go for a walk, for one thing, and she sometimes wondered if Willie Bond read the postcards.

'Why not?' said Harold Shoosmith. 'I *always* read postcards; other people's as well as my own. Damn it all, if you don't want a thing to be read you put it in an envelope!'

Someone said, rather coldly, that was exactly why she *never* used postcards. One was at the mercy of unscrupulous busybodies. Her letters were left, neatly secured with a rubber band, on the hall table to be collected by whichever Willie was on duty.

Her companion said he left his in a box in the porch. Dotty Harmer, an elderly spinster as erratic as her name implied, vouchsafed the information that she hung hers on the gate in a string bag, and that they had blown away once or twice. Significant glances were exchanged behind the lady's back. What else would you expect of Dotty?

'My new next door neighbour,' remarked Winnie Bailey

'leaves hers pinned under the knocker, I see. It must weigh seven or eight pounds. It's that great brass dolphin old Admiral Trigg fixed up years ago, you know. Nothing could get blown away from that thing!'

Suddenly, the subject of letters was dropped. Here was something of much greater importance. Who was Winnie Bailey's neighbour? Where did she come from? Would she be staying long?

The party turned expectantly towards Winnie, avid for the latest news from Thrush Green.

The house where the newcomer had recently arrived had been empty for two years. Tullivers, as it was called, had been the home of old Admiral Josiah Trigg and his sister Lucy for almost thirty years, and when he died, suddenly, one hot after-noon, after taking the sharp hill from the town at a spanking pace, his sister continued to muddle along in a vague, amiable daze, for another eighteen months, before succumbing to bronchitis.

'If it's not the dratted hill,' pronounced old Piggott the sexton gloomily, 'that carries off us Thrush Green folks, it's the dratted east wind. You gotter be tough to live 'ere.'

You certainly had to be tough to live at Tullivers after the Admiral had gone, for Lucy Trigg, in her eighties, could not be bothered to have any domestic help, nor could she be bothered to light fires, to cook meals for herself, nor to clean the house and tend the garden.

Winnie Bailey, the soul of tact, did what she could in an unobtrusive way, but knew she was fighting a losing battle. The curtains grew greyer, the window-panes misty with grime, the door-step and path were spattered with bird-droppings, and the docks and nettles rioted in the borders once tended by Lucy's brother and kept trim and shipshape with pinks, pansies and geums neatly confined within immaculate box hedges.

It wasn't as if Lucy Trigg were senile. Her mind, in some ways, was as clear as ever. She played a good game of bridge with her neighbours. She attacked, and overcame, the challenge of *The Daily Telegraph* crossword puzzle each morning, and played her dusty piano with fingers still nimble despite arthritis. It was simply that the squalour of her house did not affect her. Her world had shrunk to the few things which still had interest for her. The rest was ignored.

It was fortunate that Tullivers was a small house with a small garden. Doctor Bailey, as a young man, had been offered the major part of the next door garden by the Admiral's predecessor. He had bought it for thirty pounds, enclosed it with a honey-coloured Cotswold stone wall, and planted a small but fine orchard, now at the height of its production. Thus the Bailey's garden was L-shaped, and the remaining portion of Tullivers' land, a mere quarter of an acre, allowed room for only a lawn, a few mature lilac and may trees and the flower border which had been the Admiral's particular pride.

An Albertine rose grew splendidly over one end of the house, and winter jasmine starred the front porch in the cold of the year. Inside were two fairly small square rooms, one each side of the front door, with a roomy kitchen built on at the back.

Above stairs were two modest bedrooms and a bathroom with Victorian fittings and a geyser which made threatening rumbles, wheezes and minor explosions when in use.

Tullivers, in its heyday, was always known as 'a snug house' by Thrush Green people. It stood at right angles to the road, and rather nearer it than most of the larger houses which stood back in their well-kept gardens.

It faced south, across the Bailey's front garden, towards the roofs of Lulling in the valley below, a mile distant. It crouched there, as snug as a contented cat, catching the sunshine full on its face.

To see Tullivers so neglected had grieved Thrush Green. Its decay over the past two years had been a constant topic of conversation. It had been left to a nephew of Lucy Trigg's, also a naval man, who put it in the hands of a London estate agent to sell for him whilst he was abroad.

'Pity he didn't let the local chaps have it,' was the general opinion. 'Keep a sharper eye on it. Should have gone within the month.'

There had been one or two prospective buyers, pushing their

way through the tall weeds, with papers describing the property's charms in their hands, but the general neglect seemed to dishearten them. Heavy snow in January and February kept other possible buyers away, and by the time the crocuses and daffodils were decking the rest of the Thrush Green gardens, Tullivers was looking at its worst.

Birds nested in the porch and in the guttering, and a bold jackdaw started to build in the cold unused chimney. Mice had found shelter in the kitchen, and spiders spun their webs unmolested.

The children at the village school eyed the blank windows speculatively, and the bigger boys fingered the catapults hidden in their pockets, longing to pick up pebbles and let fly at this beautiful sitting target. What could be more exhilarating than the crack of a glass pane, the dramatic starring, the satisfying hole? Two of the most daring had been observed in the garden by Miss Watson, the headmistress, who lived across the green at the school house, and she had delivered dire warnings during assembly the next morning. The two malefactors had been displayed to the assembled school as 'Trespassers Loitering With Criminal Intent,' and were suitably abashed. Thrush Green parents, fortunately, were still unspoilt by modern educational theories and heartily approved of Miss Watson's strong line. Miss Fogerty, who was in charge of the infants' class, added her own warnings when she regained the classroom, and the infants approached their morning's labours in a suitably sober mood. It says much for the two ladies, and the parents of Thrush Green, that the little house remained safe from children's assaults, despite temptation.

One bright April day, a red Mini stopped outside Tullivers and a tall woman, paper fluttering from a gloved hand, made her way into the house.

Miss Fogerty was on playground duty that morning. Standing on the sheltered side of the school, teacup in hand, she watched with mounting excitement. Around her squealed and shouted the sixty or so pupils of Thrush Green Church of England Primary School. During those delirious fifteen

minutes of morning play-time, they were variously space-men,
horses, footballers, boxers, cowboys or – among the youthful
minority – simply mothers and fathers. The noise was ear-
splitting. The bracing Cotswold air produces fine healthy lungs
and the rumpus made at play-time could be clearly heard by
fond parents who were safely half a mile away.

Agnes Fogerty, quiet and still as a mouse, and not unlike
that timid animal in her much-pressed grey flannel skirt and
twin-set to match, stood oblivious of the chaos around her.
Somehow, she sensed that the stranger would take on Tullivers
one day. There was something purposeful about that stride
towards the front door, and the deft slipping of the key into the
lock – almost as though the house were hers already, thought
little Miss Fogerty.

And quite alone! Perhaps she was a single woman? Or
perhaps her husband was working and she had decided to look
at the place herself before they came down together? Or, of
course, she might be a widow? The war had left so many
attractive women without husbands. Miss Fogerty gave a small
sigh for all that might have been, and then remembered, sharply,
that the stranger was much younger than she was herself, and
could not have been much more than a baby during the last
war.

Not that widowhood could be dismissed quite so neatly,
Miss Fogerty comforted herself. After all, the number of young
men who succumbed to coronary thrombosis alone, not to
mention the annual toll of influenza and road casualties, was
quite formidable. On the whole, Miss Fogerty liked the idea of
a sensible widow occupying Tullivers. Who knows? She might
even become friendly with another well-read woman living
nearby, and companionable little tea-parties and visits to each
other's houses might blossom. Miss Fogerty, it will be observed
was lonely at times.

Meanwhile, time was getting on. Miss Fogerty consulted her
watch, which she hauled up on a chain from beneath her grey
jumper, and then clapped her hands for attention. It says much
for her discipline that within one minute the playground was
quiet enough for her small precise voice to be heard.

'Lead in, children,' she said, 'and *no pushing*!'

She followed the last child towards the arch of the Gothic doorway, pausing there for a last look across the green to Tullivers. The stranger had vanished from view inside the house. The dashing red mini-car waited by the kerb.

Here was something to tell dear Miss Watson! Warm with excitement, Agnes Fogerty entered her accustomed realm, the infants' room. As soon as school dinner was finished, and she and her headmistress were enjoying their cup of instant coffee, she would impart this latest snippet of news to her colleague.

Needless to say, many other people observed the stranger's entry to Tullivers. Thrush Green, to the uninitiated, might have seemed remarkably quiet that morning. The school-children apart, not more than two or three people were to be seen. There were, of course, almost a dozen unseen – hidden behind curtains, screened by garden shrubs, or cocking a curious eye from such vantage points as porches and wood sheds.

Albert Piggott, languidly grubbing up the dead winter grass at the foot of the churchyard railings, kept the stranger comfortably in view. He approved of the red Mini. Must have a bit of money to drive a car, and that great leather handbag had cost something, he shouldn't wonder. He knew a decent bit of leather when he saw it. Plastic never deceived Albert Piggott yet. A handsome gal too, with a nice pair of long legs.

Not like his old woman, he thought sourly. He straightened up slowly, eyes still fixed upon the unsuspecting stranger. What on earth had made him marry that great lump Nelly Tilling? He should have known it would never work. Women were all the same. Wheedled their way into your life, cunning as cats, and once they'd hooked you, the trouble started.

'You ain't washed, Albert! Time you took a bath, Albert! Give over sniffing, Albert! You've got plenty of hankies what want using. I wants more money than this for house-keeping. And you can keep out of the pub, Albert! That's where the money goes!'

His wife's shrill voice echoed in his head. He hadn't had a

day's peace since they were wed, and that was God's truth, said the sexton piously to himself.

Marriage never did anyone any good. He'd take a bet that that young woman at Tullivers' front door was single. She could afford to buy a house, to run a car, to keep herself looking nice. Probably one of these career women who'd had the sense to keep out of matrimony.

Albert leant moodily on the railings, a fistful of dead grass against his shirt front, and pondered on the inequality of the bounty supplied by Providence. By now, the stranger had unlocked the door and entered the house.

For the first time that morning Albert became conscious of the warmth of the sun and the song of a bold robin perched upon the tombstone of Lavinia, Wife of Robert Entwistle, Gent., who had left sunshine and birdsong behind her for ever on 3 February 1792.

Nelly might be no beauty. She was certainly a nagger. But he had just remembered that she was preparing a steak and kidney pie when he had left her an hour ago, and Nelly's hand with pastry was unsurpassed.

Cheered by this thought, and by the hopeful signs of spring about him, Albert bent again to his task. Another warming idea occurred to him. Single women often needed a hand with wood-chopping, hedge-trimming and the like. It would be a good thing to have a little extra money coming in. With any luck, he could keep it from Nelly, and spend it as he used to, in his carefree pre-marital days, at 'The Two Pheasants'!

Albert Piggott broke into a rare and rusty whistling.

But it was Ella Bembridge who had the closest look at the newcomer that morning.

She was about to cross from her cottage to the rectory on the green opposite to consult her friend Dimity Henstock about the advisability of having the boiler chimney swept.

Such mundane affairs had always been left to Dimity when the two women shared the cottage where Ella now lived alone. The rector's wife, as well as running her own ungainly house, found herself continuing to keep an eye on her old establishment, for Ella was the most impractical creature alive.

It was Dimity who defrosted Ella's refrigerator before the icy stalactites grew too near the top shelf. It was Dimity who surreptitiously threw away the fortnight-old stew which had grown a fine crop of pale blue fur upon its surface, or some shapeless mess which had started out as a fruit mousse and had collapsed into something reminiscent of frogs' spawn. She did not chide her old friend about her slap-dash ways. She loved her too well to hurt her, and recognized that Ella's warm heart and her artistic leanings more than made up for her complete lack of housewifery.

The little red car had just drawn up as Ella was slamming her gate. Ella had no scruples about staring, and she stood now, a sturdy figure, watching unashamedly as the stranger emerged.

The younger woman gave Ella no greeting, as country people are wont to do. In fact, she appeared not to notice the watching figure. She locked the car door (a precaution which most Thrush Green folk forgot to take) and consulted the paper in her hand before walking swiftly towards Tullivers.

Ella waited until the front door closed behind her with a groaning of rusty hinges, and then crossed the road to the rectory where she found Dimity in the kitchen beating up eggs whilst her husband made the mid-morning coffee.

Over their steaming cups Ella gave her account of the newcomer.

'About thirty, I reckon. Looks bright enough – might be useful in the W.I. Nice dog-tooth check suit in brown and white, and stockings with no seams. Come to think of it – they were probably tights. I didn't see any tops when she clambered out of the mini.'

'Ella dear,' protested Charles Henstock mildly. 'Spare my feelings.'

'Nice pair of square-toed shoes, Russell and Bromley probably, and an Italian handbag.'

'How on earth do you know?' expostulated Dimity.

'I can smell Italian leather a mile off,' said Ella, fishing a battered tin from her pocket and beginning to roll a cigarette from the crumpled papers and loose tobacco therein.

'And I'd take a bet her ear-rings were Italian too,' she added, blowing out an acrid cloud of smoke. Dimity quietly moved the egg-custard out of range.

'Ears pierced?' asked the rector, with rare sarcasm.

'Couldn't see,' replied Ella in a matter-of-fact tone. 'But wears good gloves.'

Something sizzled in the oven and Dimity crossed the kitchen to attend to it.

'Not that I really noticed her,' continued Ella. 'Just got a passing glimpse, you know.'

The rector forbore to comment.

'But she's welcome to Tullivers,' went on Ella. 'There's a jackdaw's nest the size of a squirrel's drey in the kitchen chimney. Which reminds me – shall I get the boiler chimney done, Dim?'

Dimity sat back on her heels by the open oven door and looked thoughtful.

'September, October, November, December, January, February, March, April – yes, Ella. Get it swept now.'

'Good,' replied her old friend, rising briskly and dropping her cigarette stub into the sink basket where it smouldered, unpleasantly close to the shredded cabbage soaking in a bowl.

'I got my old hand loom out again last night,' said Ella conversationally. 'Thought I'd run up a few ties ready for the next Bring and Buy Sale and Christmas time.'

She looked speculatively at Charles, who was doing his best to repress a shudder. He already had four ties of Ella's making, each much too short, the colour of over-cooked porridge, and far too thick to knot properly. Fortunately, he wore his clerical collar more often than not, and could safely leave the monstrosities in the drawer without hurting Ella's feelings.

'Lovely, dear,' said Dimity automatically, putting the egg-custard into the oven carefully.

'I'll see you out,' said the rector, following Ella along the cold dark passage to the front door.

Outside, Thrush Green sparkled in the bright April sunshine. It was like emerging from a dark cave in the cliffs on to a sunlit beach, thought Ella. She was thankful that she did not have to live in the rectory. Could anything ever make that north-facing pile of Victorian architecture comfortable?

She looked towards Tullivers, and the rector's gaze followed hers. The shabby little house basked in the sunshine like some small, battered, stray cat grateful for warmth.

There was no sign of the stranger, and the red car had gone.

'Oh,' cried the rector, genuinely disappointed, 'I'd hoped to catch sight of her, I must admit.'

'You will,' prophesied Ella, setting off purposefully for her own cottage. 'Mark my words, Charles Henstock, you will!'

2. *Who is She?*

TWO or three weeks later the red car reappeared. This time the young woman had a companion, as sharp eyes on Thrush Green were quick to observe.

A small boy, of about six years of age, clambered out of the car and jumped excitedly up and down on the pavement. He was a well-built child, flaxen-haired and fair-skinned, and seemed delighted with his first glimpse of Thrush Green. He pointed to Tullivers, obviously asking questions. He pointed to the fine statue of Nathaniel Patten, erected a year or two earlier by Thrush Green residents to honour one of their famous men, and he was clearly impressed by the church and the village school across the green.

The woman looked up and down the road, as though waiting for somebody. Her answers to the child appeared perfunctory.

After a few minutes, she led the way to the front door, followed by the boy. Just as it closed behind them, the local builder's battered van screeched to a halt behind the red car, and out tumbled Joe Bush.

'Late as usual!' was the general comment of the hidden onlookers of Thrush Green as they watched him scurry up the path.

By standing on tip-toe, little Miss Fogerty could just see what was going on across the green. The Gothic window was uncomfortably high, installed by its Victorian builders for just that purpose – to make sure that children could not look out easily and so be distracted from their pot-hooks and hangers by the giddy world outside.

The sand-tray was also rather awkwardly placed beneath the window. Miss Fogerty made up her mind to shift it at playtime. This week the sand-tray carried a tiny replica of Thrush Green with plasticine houses, duly labelled with their owners' names, the church, the school, and even a passable representation of

Nathaniel Patten's statue. Some of the infants had proudly brought contributions to the scene. Toy lorries, cars, and even an Army tank, had found a place on the roads across the green, and though grossly over-sized for their surroundings they made an imposing addition to the sand-tray. It was unfortunate that the fine avenue of chestnut trees which flanked the north side of the green, had also been constructed of plasticine. The heat from the hot-water pipe nearby had caused them to bow to the ground with flaccid exhaustion. Loving fingers restored them to the upright position a dozen times a day, but Miss Fogerty decided that twigs set in a plasticine base must replace the present avenue without delay.

Miss Fogerty shifted a Virol jar full of paint brushes further along the window-sill, the better to follow the stranger's activities. The little boy aroused her keenest interest. He looked just the right age for her class, and very likely he could read already. What a blessing! And could probably manage his own buttons and shoe-laces too which was more than half her class could accomplish. It was truly disgraceful that Gloria Curdle, at the great age of six, was still unable to tie a bow!

'Which reminds me,' said Miss Fogerty to herself. 'Tears or no tears, that child's tin camel *must* be removed from the Thrush Green model. Looming over the church spire is bad enough, in all conscience, but having an Asiatic creature like that among the Cotswolds scenery just Will Not Do!'

Firmly she plucked the offending beast from its alien pastures and put it safely into her sagging cardigan pocket.

Across the green the little boy was jumping rhythmically. Good coordination, noted Miss Fogerty approvingly, and plenty of spring.

'I wonder if there are any more children?' speculated Miss Fogerty. A tugging at her skirt nearly precipitated her into the sand-tray.

'Child,' cried Miss Fogerty, with unusual sharpness. 'Don't pull people about in that rude fashion.'

'I can't wait,' said the child, with simple candour.

'Be quick then,' responded Miss Fogerty automatically,

returning reluctantly to her duties, with a last glance at Joe Bush's retreating back.

'She's back again,' announced Betty Bell to her employer Harold Shoosmith.

Harold Shoosmith was a comparative newcomer himself to Thrush Green, having come to live there on his retirement from business in Africa two or three years earlier. Tall, spare and handsome ... and, best of all, a bachelor ... he was welcomed warmly by the community.

It had been his idea to honour one of Thrush Green's famous sons, the missionary Nathaniel Patten, and the splendid statue of their nineteenth century hero now graced the green.

The fact that Harold was happy to take part in village affairs, and had the leisure to do so, meant that he was on a dozen or more local committees. At this moment he was immersed in the Thrush Green Entertainments Club's accounts. He looked up from his desk. He had long since given up remonstrating with his slap-dash help about bursting into occupied rooms. If Betty Bell held a duster in her hand, she looked upon it as a passport to free passage anywhere in the house, the bathroom included. Early in their acquaintance she had bounced in to encounter her employer stark naked, except for an inadequate face flannel, but had not been a whit abashed. It was Harold Shoosmith who suffered from shock. After that, he prudently locked the door when at his ablutions.

'Who's back?' he asked apprehensively. Ella Bembridge, whom he found most trying, had just left him after delivering the parish magazine, and he feared her return.

'That new party,' responded Betty, flicking an African carving, knocking it from its shelf and catching it adroitly, all in a second. Harold, wincing, could not help admiring her deftness. Practice, he supposed, resignedly.

'Her that's coming to Tullivers,' continued Betty, attacking a small enamelled clock mercilessly. 'Got a young man with her this time,' she added archly.

'Husband, I expect,' said Harold, returning to his accounts.

'What! That age?' cried Betty, giggling at the success of her subtlety. 'He ain't no more'n six, I'll lay.'

She fell energetically upon a window sill. A dozing fly burst into a frenzy of buzzing as it tried to escape from her onslaught.

'If you was to go out the front and down to the gate you'd get a good look at her,' advised Betty. 'She's hanging about for someone. Joe Bush, I expect. That place'll need a proper going-over before it's fit to live in.'

'I shouldn't dream of staring at the lady,' said Harold sternly. 'And, in any case, I think you are taking a lot for granted. No one knows if she proposes to buy Tullivers. If she does, then we shall call in the usual way.'

Betty Bell was not affected by the touch of frost in Harold's manner. Hoity-toity was her only silent comment, as she gave a final drubbing to the window sill.

'Wantcher desk done?' she asked cheerfully.

'No thanks,' replied Harold shortly. 'I want to work on it.'

'Okay, okay!' replied his daily help. 'I'll go and put the curry on. Suit you?'

'Very well, Betty, thank you,' said Harold, his good humour restored at the thought of her temporary absence.

The door crashed behind her, and soon the sound of clashing saucepans proclaimed that his lunch was being prepared. Distracting though the noise was, Harold Shoosmith thanked heaven that it was at a distance.

He turned again to his accounts.

Across the green, young Doctor Lovell was having trouble too. The last patient at his morning surgery was Dotty Harmer.

He had to admit, in all fairness, that she did not worry him unduly with her ailments. She preferred to deal with them herself with a variety of herbal remedies ranging from harmlessly wholesome to downright dangerous, in the doctor's opinion.

His senior partner, Doctor Bailey, who was now too frail to take much part in the practice, had warned him about Dotty.

'Eccentric always – plain crazy sometimes,' he summed up succinctly. 'Father was a proper martinet, and taught at the local grammar school. His wife died young, and Dotty kept house for the old Tartar until he died. As you'll see, the place is filthy, full of animals, and the garden is a jungle of herbs from which Dotty brews the most diabolical concoctions. I beg of you, young man, never to eat or drink anything which Dotty has prepared. We have a special complaint at Thrush Green known as "Dotty's Collywobbles". Be warned!'

Since then, the young partner had frequently met those suffering from this disorder. Doctor Bailey, he realized early in their friendship, knew his patients pretty thoroughly.

This morning he examined a long angry gash in Dotty's forearm, caused by the horn of a young goat who was the latest addition to Dotty's motley family.

'Such a sweet disposition really,' said Dotty earnestly. 'It wasn't *meant*, you know. Just playfulness.'

'When was it done?' asked the doctor.

'One day last week, I think,' said Dotty vaguely. 'Or the week before, perhaps. The weeks pass so quickly, don't they? Monday morning it's Saturday afternoon, if you know what I mean. I treated it at once, of course.'

'What with?'

'Now let me see. I think it was one of dear Gerard's. From his Herball, you know. Yes, I remember now, it was All-Heale.'

'All-Heale?' asked Doctor Lovell, whose knowledge of sixteenth-century remedies was shaky.

'As a practising physician,' said Dotty sharply, 'you surely know Clownes Wound-Wort! You simply pound the leaves with a little pure lard and apply the ointment to any open wound. Gerard gives several examples of his success with the cure. I should have thought that all medical men would be conversant with the "poore man of Kent who in mowing of Peason did cut his leg with a sithe". He had the sense to apply All-Heale, and was cured within days.'

'I'll give you a shot of antibiotics,' said Doctor Lovell firmly. He scribbled a prescription, turning a deaf ear to his patient's protestations.

'The lotion should be used twice a day,' he continued,

handing her the form, 'and keep the wound covered. Take the tablets night and morning. You'll be fine in a day or two, but come back if it gives any further trouble.'

Dotty took it in her claw-like grasp and surveyed the hieroglyphics with distaste and doubt.

Doctor Lovell relented, and patted her bony shoulder.

'Most of these things are based on the tried herbal recipes, you know,' he said mendaciously.

Dotty looked relieved.

'I hope you're right, young man,' she said, opening the surgery door. Her eye lit upon the red car and Joe Bush's van.

'Have you met your new neighbour?' inquired Dotty.

'First I've heard of one,' said Doctor Lovell.

'You're the only person on Thrush Green who hasn't,' replied Dotty tartly.

Setting off for her cottage half a mile away, Dotty shook her untidy grey head over modern physicians. They seemed to know nothing about their really great forebears, and very little of the immediate world about them. It didn't give a patient much confidence, to be sure.

She fingered the prescription in her coat pocket. For two pins, she'd tear it up and forget it. But just suppose that her arm refused to heal and she was obliged to return to that silly fellow?

It might be prudent to give his nostrums a brief trial. Medical men were so touchy if one ignored their advice.

Nevertheless, as soon as she had traversed the alley by Albert Piggott's house which led to the path to Lulling Woods, and knew that she was out of sight of Thrush Green, Dotty stopped to extract a string bag from her pocket, and advanced purposefully upon a fine collection of weeds growing in the ditch.

'Best to be on the safe side,' said Dotty to herself, thrusting the pungent leaves into the bag.

Swinging it jauntily, she skipped homeward, well satisfied.

3. The Priors Meet Their Neighbours

In the months that followed, Joe Bush's van spent most of its time standing outside Tullivers. Not that the house was a hive of activity – Joe Bush's methods, and those of his two assistants, were both leisurely and erratic. There were frequent trips down the steep hill to Lulling High Street, where lay the builder's yard, for forgotten items. There were a prodigious number of 'brew-ups' during the day, so that work proceeded slowly.

Luckily, perhaps, only the basic repairs seemed to be tackled. Loose roof tiles were replaced, the jackdaw's nest removed from the kitchen chimney, and two faulty windows were rehung. Inside, a few rotting floor-boards were made good and a particularly hideous fireplace removed. Otherwise, it seemed, the house would be put into shape by its owner.

'Cor!' exclaimed Joe Bush, to the landlord of "The Two Pheasants". 'She've got plenty to do there, I'll tell you. I shan't get fat on what she's spending, and that's the truth.'

'Maybe she ain't got it to spend,' replied the landlord reasonably. 'She being a widow, I take it.'

'And what makes you think that?' asked Joe, heavily sarcastic. 'She's got a husband all right.'

'Don't show up much,' commented the landlord.

'He's overseas,' replied Joe, putting down his empty glass and making for the door. 'I shouldn't wonder,' he added vaguely.

'Either he is or he isn't,' pointed out the landlord, understandably nettled.

'Well, that's what she told the kid last week when they was down. But you knows women. Crafty as a wagon-load of monkeys. Maybe he's doin' time and she don't want the kid to know.'

'Don't talk out the back of your neck,' begged the landlord.

He flapped at the counter with a teacloth in a dismissive fashion. Joe took the hint and vanished.

The absence of a man in the stranger's life certainly intrigued Thrush Green. It was established that the handsome lady was a Mrs Prior, that her son was called Jeremy, and that they lived, at the present time, in a flat in Chelsea.

These interesting facts had been gleaned from the child, rather than from his mother, by Joe Bush's junior assistant, known as Sawny Sam locally, for obvious reasons, although his baptismal name was Samuel Ellerman John Plumb. It was Sawny Sam who held ladders, carried hods, mixed cement, wheeled barrows, fetched forgotten items from the yard, and brewed the tea six times a day.

He had a gentle, kindly disposition, and at seventeen years of age his intelligence was on a par with young Jeremy's. They got on famously, sharing a love of football, animals and stamp collecting.

On several occasions during the summer, Mrs Prior and Jeremy came down at weekends to decorate the interior of Tullivers. While his mother slapped vigorously at the walls with white emulsion paint, the child occupied himself happily in the garden. On Saturday mornings, the builders were at work, and it was then that the friendship grew between Jeremy and Sawny Sam.

'I'm going to that school,' said Jeremy, nodding across to the other side of the green.

'It's ever so nice,' said Sam heavily. 'My cousin Dave went there. He was a monitor.'

'Why didn't you go?'

'I lives up the street. I 'ad to go to St Margaret's School. We 'ad a beast of a 'ead.'

'What did he do?'

''It yer!'

'What for?'

'Anythink. Nothink.'

'He sounds cruel.'

''E were.'

'Is he still?'

'No. He's stopped now.'

'Why?'

'Dead,' said Sam perfunctorily.

He filled the kettle, and Jeremy set out the enamel mugs for the second tea-break of the day. He looked thoughtful.

'Are they cruel over there?'

'Nah!' drawled Sam derisively. 'There's only two old ducks – Miss Watson and Miss Fogerty. Like Aunties, they are. Gives you sweets and that. Friday afternoons you can take any gear you likes to play with.'

'Like stamp albums?' asked Jeremy eagerly.

'Dinky cars, if you want to. Anythink – absolutely *anythink*, Dave said. Except guns and catapults and that. Them two don't 'old with guns. Nothink dangerous.'

They sat companionably, side by side, on a low pile of bricks, and looked across at Jeremy's new school, while the kettle hummed.

'I shall like it,' announced Jeremy, with decision. 'Shall I learn things?'

Sawny Sam's mouth and eyes became three O's in astonishment.

'Learn? 'Course you'll *learn*. Them two'll learn you all right. Poitry, tables – '

'*Tables?*' exclaimed Jeremy. 'What tables? You can't *learn* tables. You eat off 'em.'

'You must go to a pretty soppy school if you ain't 'eard of tables. Multiplication tables! Twice two are four, three twos are six, four twos are eight, five twos are ten. I knows 'em all – well, nearly. Never quite mastered seven times and twelve times,' admitted Sam frankly.

'We work things out like that with milk bottles at my school,' said Jeremy.

'Must take a lotter time,' said Sam.

'And a lot of milk bottles,' responded Jeremy. They relapsed into silence, brooding vaguely upon elementary arithmetic. The kettle lid began to rattle cheerfully and Sam rose to attend to it.

'Tell you one thing,' he said. 'You'll do all right with Miss Fogerty. She learns kids a treat. Been at it a hundred years, I shouldn't wonder. My dad said so.'

It was a comforting thought.

It was that night that Winnie Bailey, next door to Tullivers, woke at two o'clock. In the other bed her husband tossed restlessly.

'Are you all right, Donald?' she asked softly.

'Sorry, my dear, to have woken you,' wheezed the old man. 'Just can't sleep, that's all.'

'I'll go and warm some milk. It will do us both good,' said Winnie, groping for her slippers. She shrugged herself into her comfortable ancient red dressing gown, and made her way downstairs. In the kitchen, as the milk warmed on the stove, she looked out upon the dark garden. In the distance, an owl screeched from Lulling Woods. A frond of jasmine tapped at the window, and turning to the noise, Winnie Bailey had a severe shock. A light was showing in Tullivers.

Could it be that someone had broken in? Could that attractive young woman have left the light switched on? Should she go and investigate? Or ring the police?

An ominous hissing from the milk saucepan interrupted her agitated thoughts. She filled two mugs, put them on a small tray, and then went to look cautiously from the front door across to her new neighbours.

To her surprise, she saw the little red car parked in the short drive to Tullivers. The light, she now perceived, was a very low one. She realized suddenly that it was a night-light, and recalled with a pang, her own children's early years, when a night-light burned comfortingly in a saucer of water to keep away those bogeys which come at night to scare the young.

But what an extraordinary thing, thought Winnie, mounting the stairs carefully. What could those two be sleeping on? And how cheerless it must be in that cold, empty house!

She had spoken once or twice to the young woman who had introduced herself as Phil Prior, but Winnie had felt that the stranger did not welcome overtures too warmly, and so she had decided to 'make haste slowly', as Donald often said. No doubt, the girl had plenty to do in the short time at her disposal on each visit, and any interruptions were frustrating.

But really, thought Winnie, she must see that those two were all right in the morning. Why on earth didn't they put up at 'The Fleece' overnight?

By the time she regained the bedroom, her husband had fallen asleep. She knew better than to disturb him. Sleep was of more value to the frail man than hot milk.

She sipped her own milk thoughtfully, turning over in her mind the conditions of the pair next door. There was something rather sad about them, she felt. Perhaps 'sad' was too strong a word to use about two young and obviously healthy people. On second thoughts, 'forlorn' fitted them better. As though they were faintly neglected – as though they had lost something desperately necessary.

Could it be, thought Winnie, a husband and a father?

She must certainly risk a snub, and speak to Mrs Prior in the morning. Putting her mug gently upon the bedside table, she slipped, within minutes, into troubled slumber.

Winnie Bailey was one of the very few residents of Thrush Green who attended the communion service at eight o'clock at St Andrew's.

No one was stirring at Tullivers as she returned to prepare breakfast, and it was almost ten o'clock before she heard the child's voice from the garden next door. The August sun was already hot, and Thrush Green was going to have a day of shimmering heat. Doctor Bailey was lying in the old wicker chaise-longue, a rug across his legs, and a battered panama hat tilted over his eyes.

He wished, for the thousandth time, that he was not such a useless crock. Doctor Lovell and Winnie had to work far too hard for his liking. There was no doubt about it, the time was fast arriving when young Lovell would need another partner, and a pretty active one too.

A new estate was growing rapidly along the lane leading to

Nod and Nidden. Two or three dozen families had moved in already, mainly young couples with one or two babies, and obviously more would come. The practice had almost doubled in size since he arrived there with Winnie in their young days.

How happy they had been, he thought! His mind dwelt on early patients, many now dead, and the welcome they had given him. He remembered, with affection, the matriarchal figure of Mrs Curdle, the gipsy woman who ran the annual one-day fair on Thrush Green every first of May. He hoped that young Ben, her grandson, who was now in charge, would call again next May.

His eye fell upon his pale wasted hands, and he wondered, without self-pity, if he could live long enough to see the fair again. He doubted it. As a medical man, he could gauge his future fairly accurately. Already, he told himself, he was living on borrowed time. And how good it was! Despite weakness and pain, life was still precious, and the companionship of Winnie the mainspring of his days.

He saw her now crossing the garden to the hedge, and heard the little boy from Tullivers answering her questions. Very soon a third voice was added to the conversation, but he could not distinguish the words.

Winnie came up to him and tucked the rug neatly round his legs.

'I've asked our new neighbours to come and have coffee,' she told him. 'It won't tire you?'

'Attractive women never tire me,' said her husband gallantly.

An hour later they arrived.

'Please forgive my piebald appearance,' said the young woman, gazing down at her black jeans and sleeveless black blouse. Both were liberally speckled and streaked with white paint. 'It seems to run down my arm and trickle off my elbow.'

'Try a roller,' advised the doctor.

'I simply can't manage one,' confessed the girl, and the comparative merits of brushes and rollers occupied them happily whilst Mrs Bailey went to fetch the tray, accompanied by a chattering Jeremy.

'And when do you hope to move in?'

'In two or three weeks, with luck. The men should have finished by then, they say.'

'Yes – well,' said the doctor, rubbing his bony nose doubtfully. 'That may be so, but if I were you I should move in even if they haven't departed. Joe Bush takes his time.'

'It hadn't escaped me,' replied the young woman, smiling. Mrs Bailey returned with the tray.

'We've got *two* sorts of biscuits,' announced Jeremy excitedly.

'It's not very polite to comment on other people's food,' his mother told him gently.

'It sounded favourable comment to me,' said Winnie. 'We like that here.'

'We had rather a scratch breakfast,' said Mrs Prior. 'We stayed overnight for the first time.'

Winnie was glad that she had mentioned the burning subject first.

'Were you both comfortable?' she asked.

'Hardly. Our camp beds are the sort that Victorian explorers humped about!'

'Or probably their native bearers humped about,' suggested Doctor Bailey.

'Are they hard?' asked Winnie anxiously. 'We have two spare feather-beds. Or better still, come and sleep here. You would be quite free to come and go when you pleased.'

'You're very kind,' said the girl. She flushed in a way that made her look suddenly young and defenceless.

'Or "The Fleece" is very comfortable, I know,' went on Winnie, intent upon her visitors' well-being.

'Too expensive,' said the girl.

'Hotel prices are ruinous these days,' agreed the doctor. 'Sugar, Mrs Prior?'

'No, thank you. And as we're to be neighbours, do you think you could call me Phil?'

'That would be very nice. Short for Phyllis, I take it? One of my favourite names,' said Doctor Bailey.

'I wish it were.'

'Philippa?' asked Winnie.

'Worse still. My proper name is Phyllida. My parents were hopelessly romantic.'

'Henry Austin Dobson,' said the doctor. 'Born 1840, died 1921.'

'How on earth did you know?'

'My mind is full of completely useless bits and pieces, such as that,' he replied. 'But the things I want to remember – where I left my pipe, or if I gave my partner a certain urgent message, for instance – completely escape me.'

'Well, you're dead right about Austin Dobson. My parents were great readers of poetry and had a weakness for the light fantastic.'

'A pleasant change from the heavy dismal we suffer from everywhere today,' commented Winnie. 'No one seems to laugh any more.'

'I do,' said Jeremy. 'I laugh a lot.'

'Keep it up,' advised the doctor. 'Keep it up.'

'My daddy makes me laugh.' He turned to his mother. 'Doesn't he make me laugh?' he persisted.

'He certainly does,' agreed his mother.

'When's he coming to see the new house?' asked the boy, through a mouthful of ginger biscuit.

'Sometime,' said his mother evasively. She produced a crumpled handkerchief from her jeans' pocket and gave a deft dab at her son's mouth.

'My husband has to be abroad a great deal,' she explained. 'He's in a textile firm. I'm afraid Jeremy hasn't seen much of him this last week or two.'

'More like a month,' began Jeremy.

'It always seems longer than it is,' his mother said swiftly. She looked at a massive wrist-watch.

'Time we went back to our paint pots, young man,' she told him, rising. 'Thank you so much for the coffee. We shall work twice as fast after that.'

Winnie accompanied her to the gate.

'Now, don't forget. If you want to stay overnight, do let us help. We look forward to having you as neighbours.'

'We look forward to coming,' replied the girl. 'A London

flat is no place to bring up a growing boy. I was country-bred myself. I know what Jeremy's missing.'

'You'll be happy at Thrush Green,' Winnie assured her. The girl's mouth quivered.

'I'm sure we shall,' she said. 'We'll be here in good time for Jeremy to start school there in September.'

The two women looked across the green. The dew was drying rapidly, and from St Andrew's came the sound of country voices raised in praise. A pigeon clattered out from the avenue of chestnut trees, and landed nearby, strutting aimlessly this way and that, thrusting out its bright coral feet.

The girl sighed.

'It's all very comforting,' she said softly, as though speaking to herself. 'And now we must go home. Thank you again.'

They parted with smiles, and Winnie watched the pair run to Tullivers. It was good to see the little house in use again.

She returned to her own garden thoughtfully. Why did the girl use the word 'comforting' about Thrush Green? From what pain did she seek relief? From what torment was she flying? Who could tell?

4. *A Shock For Dotty*

HALF a mile away, Dotty Harmer was in trouble. She had gone down the garden to feed her hens, when she saw something move behind the garden shed.

An open-ended extension had been built on to house Dotty's winter store of logs. An energetic nephew, staying for a week of his vacation, had obligingly set some flag-stones at the entrance, so that his aunt could step from the path to the logs without getting her feet wet.

'Very nice, dear,' she had commented. 'And I can chop up the logs there. And marrow bones. So useful to have what my dear father used to call "an area of hard standing". It will be most useful, dear boy.'

Its use at the moment, when Dotty stood transfixed, henfood in hand, was unorthodox. For, lying in the sun, was a mother cat suckling five well-grown babies.

Charming though the sight was, Dotty's jaw dropped. How on earth could she cope with six cats – nay, six *more* cats! Already she owned two, a mother and daughter which she had prudently had spayed. What would they have to say about this brazen intruder and her progeny?

Dotty peered through her steel-rimmed spectacles at the family. They were a motley crew, to be sure, but how engagingly pretty! The mother was black with white paws, and one of the kittens had the same colouring. There was a fine little tabby, and three tortoiseshell kittens.

Dotty's heart sank again. Ten to one the tortoiseshells would be female. How long before their first litters arrived? Something must be done before the place was over-run with wild cats.

She took a resolute step forward, and the kittens shot into the stack of logs and vanished. One young quivering triangular tail showed for an instant in a gap, and then was gone. The mother cat crouched defensively, facing Dotty, strategically placed between this enemy and her babies. She was pathetically thin and dusty, and Dotty's tender heart went out to this gallant battered small fighter.

'Good puss! Nice little puss!' said Dotty, advancing gently.

The cat retreated slightly, and spat defiance.

Dotty put down the hen food and returned to the house for a dish of milk. Through the kitchen window she witnessed a remarkable sight. The mother cat gave a curious chirruping sound, and the five babies tumbled from the logs, towards the steaming hen food. Within seconds six heads were in the pot, as the cats ate ravenously.

Dotty stood aghast .That cats, so fastidious as a rule, should fling themselves upon cooked peelings, meat scraps and bacon rinds, all bound together with bran, showed to what excess of hunger the poor things were driven.

She watched them lick the pot clean, their eyes half-closed with bliss, and then sit down to wash themselves.

'Well, that's the last of the chicken's mash,' said Dotty aloud, and philosophically reached for the bag of corn instead. Bearing this and the brimming dish of milk she went once more down the garden path. As before, the kittens vanished, but the mother cat stood her ground. Dotty fed the hens, put down the milk, and retreated to the house, there to work out the best way to cope with an embarrassment of cats.

It was a problem which was to puzzle her, and the rest of Thrush Green, for weeks to come.

One still, hot morning, in the week following Dotty's discovery, Albert Piggot was digging a grave. For this melancholy task Albert's glum expression seemed particularly suited; but although the occasion was a sad one, it was not the circumstances of his labours that troubled Albert that morning, but the worsening conditions of his own matrimonial affairs.

He was the first to admit that he was cunningly hooked at the outset. There were a few aspects of married life which, in all fairness, he would agree were an improvement on the single state, for a man in his position. His house was warm and clean. His clothes were washed and mended. And his meals – ah, his meals! – were superb.

But once you'd said that, Albert told himself, squinting along the side of the grave for any unsightly irregularities, you'd said the lot. Nagging, whining and money-grubbing, that's what Nell was, and lately he had detected a new unpleasant note in her diatribes. There was far too much about that oil-man who came with his clanking van every other Thursday, for Albert's liking. A smarmy fellow, if ever there was one, a proper sissy, a regular droopy-drawers! And Nell was taken in by his soft soap, the great fool, and talked about it being 'so nice to see a gentleman for a change, and what a pity it was she had married beneath her'.

Albert set his spade to one side, pushed back his greasy cap and mopped his sweating brow. It was about time Sam Curdle arrived to give him a hand. He could do with it. Cotswold clay makes heavy digging in any weather. On a blazing August morning it was doubly intractable.

Sam Curdle, grandson of Mrs Curdle who once ruled over the Fair, had been released from gaol early in the New Year. Most of Thrush Green thought, and said openly, that Sam Curdle had a nerve to return to the place where he had so misbehaved.

'How he can face that poor Miss Watson he stole from, and battered into the bargain, I really don't know,' they told each other indignantly. 'It's a pity he doesn't take himself off, with that blowsy Bella of his, and find a living elsewhere.'

But that is just what Sam was incapable of doing. Here, in Thrush Green, as well he knew, were a few soft-hearted souls who would give him a little work for the sake of the children – and a *little* work was all that Sam Curdle wanted. Bella had found a daily job at a farm at Nidden while he was doing time, and had developed into a passably good worker under the brisk direction of the farmer's wife. They still lived in the battered caravan, converted years ago from a bus, in a sheltered corner of the stackyard. Here the Curdles reckoned themselves well off, with water from an outside tap, free milk, and a dozen or so cracked eggs weekly.

'You can stay there as long as you go straight,' the farmer had told Sam. 'But you try any of your gyppo tricks here, nicking eggs, knocking off the odd hen, and that sort of lark, and you get the boot, pronto!'

And Sam had toed the line.

The rector had found him odd jobs to do, both in his own garden and in the churchyard. Albert Piggott was glad to have an assistant when it came to such tasks as grave-digging and coke-sweeping. The fact that Sam Curdle was a wrongdoer and had been in prison troubled the sexton not at all.

It was Albert himself, in fact, who had helped to bring him to justice. If anything, Albert felt now a certain proprietorial warmth towards the local malefactor. Just bad luck he'd been caught. He'd simply met a master mind, was Albert's opinion. Plenty of people were quite as bad as Sam, but got away with it.

A shadow fell athwart the grave and Albert looked up to see Sam's face peering down at him.

'And about time too,' grunted Albert. He indicated the second shovel with a jerk of his black thumb.

Sam jumped down and began scraping some crumbs of earth together in a languid manner.

'Don't strain yourself,' said Albert tartly.

Sam stirred himself to attack the other end of the grave with rather more vigour. They shovelled together in silence.

A robin hopped about the growing pile of soil looking for worms. The morning sounds of Thrush Green were muffled by the height of the earth walls about them, but in the distance they could hear the children playing on the two swings on the green. There was a rhythmic squeaking as the chains swung to and fro, and occasionally the thud of the see-saw and the cries of excited children.

The two men worked steadily until St Andrew's clock struck twelve above them.

'That's it then,' said Albert, clambering painfully out of the grave. Sam followed him.

'Time for a quick 'en?' asked Sam.

'Who pays?'

'We goes Dutch.'

'Humph!' snorted Albert, but he quickened his pace,

nevertheless, as he shambled towards the open door of 'The Two Pheasants'.

But his thirst was not to be slaked immediately, for, directly in his path, stood Dotty Harmer.

'I shan't keep you,' said Dotty briskly, eyeing the pair. 'But I want you to let me know if you hear of anyone wanting a kitten.'

'Well, now miss—' began Albert.

'I know you have a cat,' cut in Dotty. Her tone implied, rightly, that she felt sorry for it. She looked at Sam Curdle with distaste.

'And I know you haven't room for one in the caravan,' she told him dismissively. 'The thing is, I have five to dispose of.'

Sam's face lit up.

'I'd be pleased to drown 'em for you, miss. Any time.'

Dotty looked at him sharply.

'Out of the question. They are far too big to drown.'

'You wouldn't catch 'em anyway,' gloomed Albert. 'Them wild cats never gets caught. Where've you got 'em?'

Dotty told him.

'Never get 'em out o' there,' said Albert, with relish. 'Why, I recollect that there was a widder woman over Lulling Woods way who had two – *just two*, mark you – livin' in her logs, and within the year she'd got *eighteen* kittens!'

'That's why I intend to tame them,' said Dotty firmly. 'I am going to get the mother cat spayed as soon as she has confidence in me.'

'You'll be lucky!' growled Albert. 'Best by far have a cat shoot and get done with the lot.'

'Disgraceful!' snapped Dotty.

'You won't never tame 'em, miss,' Sam said, hoping for five shillings, if not by drowning, then by a little erratic marksmanship.

'I should set a dog on 'em,' advised Albert. 'Rout 'em out, like, and then shoot 'em as they run away.'

'Have you thought,' asked Dotty severely, 'that they might simply be *maimed*, and not killed outright?'

'They'd die eventual,' said Albert casually.

'I am not proposing to harm these kittens, in any way whatsoever,' said Dotty, now dangerously calm. 'I shall do my best to get them tame enough to be accepted into good homes. *Good* homes!' she repeated firmly.

'I am on my way to Mrs Young to see if she will be able to have one,' she added, nodding to one of the five houses behind the chestnut avenue. 'All I wanted to ask you was to let me know if you hear of anyone needing a kitten.'

'Right, miss,' said Albert with rare deference. His dirty finger rose of its own volition to his greasy cap. Plain potty Miss Harmer was, and no doubt about it – but she was still gentry, and some innate, long-stifled instinct to acknowledge the fact had twitched Albert's hand to its unaccustomed position.

'Yes, miss,' added Sam meekly. 'I'll bear it in mind, miss.'

They entered 'The Two Pheasants' for their long awaited drink, the kittens already forgotten.

But Dotty, striding purposefully towards Joan Young's house, seethed with indignation.

'Drowning! Shooting! Setting a dog on them! A pity those two have never heard of reverence for life. I should like to have introduced them to Albert Schweitzer.'

She thought again.

'Or better still, my dear father. He'd have given them the horse-whipping they deserve!'

She reached the Young's gate.

'How I do hate cruelty!' said Dotty aloud, making for the front door.

Joan Young was the wife of a local architect. Her sister Ruth, who was lunching with her that day, was married to Doctor Lovell who, at that moment, was attending a cantankerous old bachelor of ninety-two to the south of Lulling.

Lunch was set in the large sunny kitchen. Paul Young was already at the table, waiting impatiently with the voracious hunger of a young schoolboy for the chicken which had just been lifted from the oven.

Opposite him, in his own old high chair, sat his baby cousin Mary banging lustily with her spoon.

'What's that?' asked Paul, as the bell of the front door rang sharply.

'Wozzat?' echoed his cousin, not caring particularly, but glad to try out a new expression.

'Oh, damn!' said Joan, tugging the fork from the bird. 'You carry on, Ruth, while I see to this.'

'You shouldn't swear,' reproved her son. 'Miss Fogerty made Chris wash his mouth out with soapy water once because he swore.'

'Sorry, sorry!' cried his mother, struggling with her apron strings. 'It slipped out.'

'Oh, damn!' echoed the baby thoughtfully. 'Oh, damn!'

The two sisters exchanged resigned looks, but had the wisdom not to comment. The bell split the air again, and Joan hurried to the door.

'Oh, do come in, Miss Harmer,' she cried, doing her best to sound welcoming. Who else but Dotty, she wondered, would call at twenty past twelve, and be clad, on a boiling hot day, in a tweed coat with a fur collar, topped by a purple velour hat, thick with dust, and decorated with a fine diamond brooch which, as Joan knew, had been in the family for generations and, amazingly enough, had not yet been lost by its present scatter-brained owner.

'Will you have a glass of sherry?' asked Joan, ushering her guest into the drawing-room.

'No, thank you, dear. I shall have a glass of rhubarb and ginger wine with my lunch. I find I get so sleepy if I mix my drinks midday.'

She looked sharply about the room.

'No cat?' said Dotty.

'No. Just Flo, the old spaniel, you know.'

'Well,' began Dotty, undoing her coat and settling herself. 'I'll tell you why I've come.'

Joan listened patiently to the saga of the kittens, half her mind on the fast-cooling lunch.

'And so it is essential that I wean the kittens, first and foremost,' she heard her visitor saying. 'Mr Fortescue says he can't possibly operate until the mother cat is *absolutely dry*.'

Dotty embarked on an involved obstetrical account about nursing felines, showing a remarkable grip on the subject for a spinster, thought Joan.

Her attention wandered again, only to be riveted suddenly when she heard Dotty putting a straight question.

'So how many kittens would you like?'

'Heavens!' exclaimed Joan. 'I must think about this! I don't know that Flo would care about a kitten—'

'Be a companion for her,' said Dotty firmly. 'What about Ruth? She'd like one, wouldn't she?'

'I'll ask her,' promised Joan meekly. To her relief, Dotty rose, and began to make her way to the door.

'Well, dear, I hope that's two kittens settled. It's quite a problem. I refuse to allow them to go to any but the nicest homes.'

'Thank you,' said Joan faintly.

'They won't be ready for a month or so,' continued Dotty, now on the doorstep. Joan rallied her failing senses.

'I will ring you before the end of the week,' she promised, 'and let you know if Ruth and I can have one each.'

'And tell your friends,' shouted Dotty from the gate. 'Those that are *definite cat-lovers*.'

Joan nodded her agreement, and watched her eccentric neighbour trotting briskly homeward to her rhubarb and ginger wine.

'What was all that about?' asked Ruth, when she returned to the kitchen.

'I'll tell you later,' said Joan. 'Little pitchers, you know.'

'Have big ears,' said her son. 'It was Miss Harmer, wasn't it? Did she tell you about her kittens? Chris told me. Isn't it smashing?'

He paused, and his mother watched, with mingled amusement and dismay, the light which suddenly broke out upon his countenance.

'Did she say we can have one, mummy? Did she? Oh, *please* let's! Oh, mummy, *do* let's have one! Please, please!'

Albert Piggott, much refreshed, set out from 'The Two

Pheasants' to his nearby cottage. An aroma of boiling bacon wafted towards him as he approached.

Mellowed already by a pint of bitter, Albert's spirits were cheered still further by the thought of pleasures to come. Maybe Nell wasn't such a bad sort, after all!

At that moment, a clattering van appeared at the top of the steep hill from Lulling, and Albert's heart turned once more to stone.

'Oilmen!' He spat viciously into the hedge.

'Women!' He spat again.

Albert Piggott was back to normal.

5. A Problem for Winnie

A RARE spell of superb harvest weather was broken early in September by a day of violent rainstorms. Naturally enough, it was the very day on which Mrs Prior and her son moved into Tullivers.

Gusts of wind shook veils of rain across Thrush Green. Sheets of water spread across the ground which was baked hard by weeks of sunny weather. A small river gurgled down the hill to Lulling, and the avenue of chestnut trees dropped showers of raindrops and blown leaves.

Those unfortunate enough to have to brave the weather, routed out long-unused mackintoshes, umbrellas and wellington boots, and splashed their way dejectedly across the green, sparing a sympathetic glance for the removal men, staggering from their van into Tullivers with rain-spattered furniture.

Within the little house Jeremy and his mother did their best to create order from chaos. It was no easy task, for as fast as they wheeled an armchair to its allotted place, a tea-chest would arrive to be dumped in its way.

'Where d'you want this, ma'am?' was the cry continuously, as the men appeared, far too quickly for the poor woman's comfort, with yet another bulky object.

She had thought, when packing up the belongings in Chelsea, that each tea-chest and large piece of furniture had been labelled. As in most moves, only half seemed to bear their place of destination, and soon the kitchen was beginning to become the resting place of all those boxes needing investigation.

'It's like a shop,' said Jeremy happily, surveying the scene.

'Or a lost property office,' said his mother despairingly.

At that moment, Mrs Bailey appeared.

'I'm not even going to offer to help,' she said. 'I should be quite useless. But do please both come to lunch. It's only cottage pie, but I'm sure you'll be ready for a break when the men have gone.'

She put up her umbrella again in a flurry of raindrops, waved cheerfully, and set off through the downpour.

By one o'clock the removal van had rumbled away, and Mrs Prior and Jeremy sat thankfully at the doctor's hospitable table.

'I feel as if I'd been through a washing machine,' said the girl. 'Thoroughly soaked, then tumble-dried. I'll never move again!'

'Goody-goody!' commented her son. 'I don't ever want to move away from here.'

'I certainly hope you won't,' replied Mrs Bailey, handing vegetable dishes. 'Runner beans? They're from the garden.'

'That's something I must do,' said the girl. 'I intend to grow as many vegetables as possible. There are some currant and gooseberry bushes in the garden at Tullivers, I see.'

'You may have to replace them,' said the doctor, toying with his tiny helping. 'They must be pretty ancient.'

'Do fruit bushes cost much?'

There was a note of anxiety in the girl's voice which did not escape the doctor's ear.

'More than they used, no doubt. If I were you, I should clear away all those weeds and long grass around them, fork the ground and put in plenty of bone meal. Then see if they give you a decent crop next season. If they do, well and good. If not, out with 'em!'

The girl nodded thoughtfully, acknowledging his advice. Mrs Bailey, watching her eat her cottage pie, noticed how exhausted she looked. It was understandable: the two had made an early start, and a moving day was always bone-wearying. But she seemed thinner, and there were shadows under the lovely eyes, as though she had slept poorly for many nights. Mrs Bailey's motherly heart went out to this quiet young woman in her trouble – for trouble she guessed, correctly, that she had in abundance. But this was no time to force any confidences. Perhaps, one day, the girl would feel ready to speak, and then would be the time for understanding.

At the end of the meal, the girl and her son rose to go.

'It has been simply lovely. You've really restored us both. But now we must go back and tackle the muddle.'

'Thank you for having us,' said Jeremy politely. He stood soberly eyeing the doctor's wife for a few moments, then flung his arms round her waist and gave her a tremendous hug.

'You *are* nice!' he cried. 'Like my granny!' His face was alight with happiness.

Mrs Bailey ruffled the flaxen hair, more touched than she cared to admit.

'Then I *must* be nice,' she agreed. 'Come and see me whenever you like. And put up your umbrella in the porch, or you'll be washed away before you reach home.'

She watched them splash down the path, and then caught sight of Willie Marchant, the postman, tacking erratically back and forth uphill. His black oilskins ran with water, and drops fell from the peak of his cap on to the mackintosh which covered his parcels.

He pulled in to the kerb, propped up his bicycle amidst a shower of drops, and extracted a letter from a bundle.

'One for you, Mrs Bailey,' he grunted gloomily. 'Marvellous, ain't it? Got twice as many this afternoon just because it's raining cats and dogs. That's life, ain't it?'

Mrs Bailey agreed, accepting the letter and studying it with drooping spirits.

Richard again! Now what on earth did he want?

Richard was her sister's boy, and Winnie Bailey had to confess that he was her least favourite nephew. He had always seemed mature, self-centred, and rather smug. Perhaps if he had been blessed with brothers and sisters this unchildlike quality of self-possession would have been mitigated. As it was, as an only child, Winnie Bailey found him uncannily precocious, and at times a trifle supercilious.

As he grew from babyhood to childhood, it was apparent that Richard would make his mark in the world. He was highly intelligent, hard-working, and as efficient on the games field as in the classroom. His school reports were glowing. His parents adored him, and he appeared to be popular with his school fellows. But secretly to his aunt, he was always 'that odd boy'.

To Winnie and her husband he was always punctiliously polite when he saw them. But, thought Winnie, surveying the envelope in her hand, Richard had never given her a warm-hearted hug as young Jeremy had just done!

He had obtained a First in Physics at Oxford, and spent a year or two in America collecting further honours. As he grew older, his manner had become rather more sociable, and his somewhat anaemic looks had blossomed into wiry sparseness as maturity and a passion for walking grew upon him.

He was now a man of thirty-two, engaged upon research so divorced from the ordinary scheme of things that Winnie Bailey and her husband found themselves unable to compre-hend the language, let alone the aims, of Richard's studies. They saw little of him, for his travels and lecturing commit-ments were extensive. Doctor Bailey heard of each academic success with coolness.

'Nothing wrong with his head,' was his comment, 'but he's no heart.'

Perhaps, thought Winnie, making her way to the drawing-room and her reading glasses, that is why she had never really warmed to Richard, but she kept these feelings to herself.

The doctor slept in the afternoon, and it was almost tea-time before she could hand him Richard's letter. The rain still fell relentlessly, drumming upon the roofs of Thrush Green, and drenching the schoolchildren as they straggled from the school porch. Their cries mingled with the spatter of rain on the window panes of the quiet room, as the doctor read the letter.

'Wants something, as usual,' he commented drily. Winnie remembered that this had been her own first unworthy re-action.

'What do you think?'

'It's up to you, my dear. If you feel that you would like to have him here while he is engaged on this particular work at Oxford, then go ahead. But it all means more for you to do, and I'm enough of a burden, I feel.'

'I don't like to refuse him,' began Winnie doubtfully. 'And we've plenty of room.'

She wandered to the window and looked out upon the rain-lashed garden. A few leaves, torn from the lime tree, hopped bird-like about the grass in the onslaught. On the flagged path, shiny with rain, a tawny dead sycamore leaf skidded about on its bent points, like some demented crab. The garden was alive with movement, as branches tossed, flowers quivered, grass shuddered, and drops splashed from roofs and hedges.

Winnie Bailey gazed unseeingly upon its wildness, turning over this problem in her mind. Richard, after all, was her nephew, she told herself – probably rather hard up, and simply asking for a bed and the minimum of board. Perhaps, for a little while—?

'Shall I invite him for a fortnight to see how we all manage?' she asked her husband, now deep in *The Times* crossword puzzle.

'By all means, if you would like to.'

'It wouldn't be a nuisance to you?'

'Of course not. I don't suppose I shall see much of the fellow, anyway, and he was always a quiet sort of chap about the house.'

Winnie sighed, partly with relief and partly because she had a queer premonition that something unusual – something disquieting – might come from Richard's visit.

Time was to prove her right.

During the next week or so the inhabitants of Thrush Green observed their new resident with approval. They watched her tackling Tullivers' neglected garden with considerable energy. The smoke from her bonfire billowed for two days and nights without ceasing, as hedge-trimmings, dead grass, long-defunct cabbage stalks and other kitchen-garden rubbish met their end.

The flagged path was sprinkled with weed-killer, and the hinge mended on the gate which had hung slightly awry for three years, wearing a scratched arc on the flag-stone each time the gate was opened or shut.

The gate was also given a coat or two of white paint, and the front door as well. The girl's efforts were generally approved, and Jeremy too was considered an exceptionally well-brought-up little boy.

But the continued absence of Mr Prior was, of course, a cause of disappointment and considerable speculation among the newcomer's neighbours at Thrush Green. He was obliged to be abroad for a few months, went one rumour, getting orders for his firm – variously described as one dealing in French silk, Egyptian cotton, Italian leather and Burmese teak.

Others knew, for a fact, that he was a specialist in television equipment, computers, road-surfacing, bridge-building and sewage works. Betty Bell, however, had it on the highest authority (her own) that he had something to do with advertising, and went overseas to show less advanced countries the best way to sell ball-point pens, wigs, food-mixers, plastic gnomes for the garden, and other necessary adjuncts to modern living.

Albert Piggott, on the other hand, thought that he was probably in hospital with a lingering complaint which would keep him there for many months to come. He said as much to his fat wife Nelly, whose response was typical.

'Trust you to think that, you old misery! More like he's run off with some lively bit. That wife of his don't look much fun to me!'

It certainly seemed nearer the target than some of the wild rumours. Winnie Bailey, who knew her neighbour better than the rest of Thrush Green's inhabitants, had come to much the same conclusion, but kept it to herself.

Young Doctor Lovell, who occasionally caught a glimpse of the newcomer from his surgery window, also wondered if the girl had parted permanently from her husband, and felt sorry for her vaguely forlorn appearance. He spoke about her to Ruth, his wife, and she pleased him by replying:

'Joan and I are going to see her this afternoon. Paul and her little boy would probably get on very well together, and she might be lonely, even if she is up to her eyes in getting that place straight.'

The two sisters were not the only people to welcome Phil Prior. The rector, of course, called a few days after she had arrived, his chubby face glowing with the warmth and kindness he felt for all he met, even such stony-faced parishioners as his own sexton. Ella Bembridge called, bearing a bunch of Michaelmas daisies tied with what appeared to be a length of discarded knicker elastic, and an invitation to 'blow in any time you feel like it'. Harold Shoosmith spoke to the girl over the wall while she was hacking down some formidable stinging nettles, and offered a hand with any heavy clearing up which she might encounter.

Within a fortnight she found that she knew quite well at least two dozen people nearby, and was on speaking terms, country-fashion, with every other soul who passed. When Dimity Henstock called to invite her to a small dinner party, she looked forward to getting to know her Thrush Green neighbours even better.

'But I shall have to find a baby-sitter,' she said, after thanking Dimity. She looked completely at a loss.

'It's all arranged,' Dimity told her. 'Dr Bailey does not go out these days and dear Winnie will be staying in too. She says she will look after Jeremy and Donald that evening, and thoroughly enjoy it.'

'You are all so kind. I shall look forward to it,' the girl said.

And Dimity, who had brought her modest invitation half-expecting to find someone used to much more sophisticated entertainment went away knowing positively that young Mrs Prior was quite sincere in her expressions of pleasure.

On her way back to the rectory, she called into her former home to see her old friend Ella, whom she found standing on a chair far too frail to support her bulky twelve stone of solid flesh. She was struggling to hang a curtain.

'Shan't be a minute, Dim,' she puffed. 'Got too many hooks for the rings, as usual.'

'I'll do it,' said Dimity automatically. Ella thumped heavily to the floor, and Dimity took her place on the chair.

As her neat fingers worked quickly at the muddle created by her friend, she told her about her visit to Tullivers.

'And it really looks a proper home,' she added.

'What d'you expect?' cried Ella, a note of truculence in her voice.

'A single woman can make a comfortable home just as well

as a married one. Don't need a man cluttering up the place to make *a home*!' she boomed.

From her perch, Dimity gave an all-embracing glance at yesterday's ashes in the grate, a vase of withered roses and the soft veil of dust upon the furniture.

'You're quite right dear,' she said meekly, threading the last hook into place.

6. *A Dinner Party at Thrush Green*

THE 'Fuchsia Bush', which stands well back from the road in Lulling High Street, prides itself on its home-made cakes and artistic furnishings. It is Lulling's only tea-shop, and having no competitor it tends to be a trifle smug.

Ella Bembridge, smoking one of her untidy hand-rolled cigarettes as she waited for her coffee to cool, looked with lack-lustre eye upon the 'Fuchsia Bush's' décor.

The walls had been freshly painted in an unhappy shade of lilac, and the new curtains were purple. The two waitresses wore the habitual garb of the establishment, overalls of pale mauve, with collar, lapels and belt in a dreadful shade of puce. These garments, faded from much washing, now clashed sadly with the new furnishings, and a pot of real fuchsias, on the table by the door, struggled to make the point that what Nature can do successfully cannot always be copied by Man.

A plastic tumbler, pretending to be made of glass, held a sheaf of mauve paper napkins a few inches from Ella's nose. Disgusted, she moved it to a neighbouring table, just as Dotty Harmer entered.

'Come and have a cup of this ghastly drink – coffee I *will not* call it,' shouted Ella cheerfully. The waitresses exchanged supercilious glances. How common could you get? You'd have thought a lady like Miss Bembridge would have had better manners, their look said clearly.

'Thank you, dear. Yes, a cup of coffee,' said Dotty, pulling up one thick speckled stocking which was forming a concertina over the lower part of her skinny leg. A commercial traveller, coffee cup arrested half way between table and moustache, watched with fascinated horror.

'Was going to bob down and see you,' said Ella.

'Eggs?' queried Dotty.

'No, no. Milk.'

'Why, hasn't the milkman called?'

'He's called all right,' said Ella grimly, grinding the stub of her cigarette into the Benares brass ashtray. 'But he won't be calling again.'

'Why not?'

'Because it's not milk he's delivering, but muck!'

Ella began to throw a small heap of tobacco upon a cigarette paper and roll yet another cigarette.

'Whitewash!' she continued vehemently. 'He calls it "Homogenized – ma'am".' Ella's voice rose to a squeaky falsetto as she mimicked her terrified milkman's tone.

'No cream on it at all. What's a woman to put in her coffee?'

'I take mine black,' said Dotty. Ella brushed aside this irrelevancy.

'It's perfectly horrible. No proper taste of milk, fiendishly white, like liquid paper! No! More like that stuff they make you drink in hospital, to see your innards. Begins with S.'

'Barium,' said Dotty, inspecting the plate of cakes.

'That's it – barium! Well, I'm not standing for it. I want milk that *is* milk, with cream on top and honest milk all the way down to the bottom of the jug. Can you spare some?'

'I can't make up my mind,' said Dotty thoughtfully, 'which is less indigestible – a Danish pastry or a doughnut.'

'Danish pastry,' said Ella promptly. Indecision nearly drove her mad.

Dotty took it reluctantly.

'I prefer the doughnut,' said Ella, transferring it swiftly to her own plate. 'I'm slimming.'

'Then you shouldn't be eating at all,' replied Dotty tartly, justifiably irritated by Ella's manoeuvres.

'Shock treatment,' Ella informed her blandly. She lodged her smoking cigarette across the ashtray, and attacked the doughnut energetically.

'I've only got goat's milk,' said Dotty, after a few minutes munching. 'I could spare you a pint a day. Dear Daisy is producing splendidly at the moment, but I have one or two regular customers, as you know, and the kittens are heavy drinkers just now. I'm trying to wean them.'

'I thought you had two goats,' said Ella, wiping sugar from her mouth with a man's khaki handkerchief.

'Dulcie is too young yet,' began Dotty primly. 'She hasn't been mated. After the kids are born—'

'Oh, spare me the obstetric details!' begged Ella. 'A pint of Daisy's daily, would be a godsend, Dotty, if you can spare it. I'll collect, of course. When can we start?'

'This afternoon? After tea?'

'Fine,' said Ella, thrusting her wheel-back chair from the table with an ear-splitting grating on the flagged floor.

'Have you got some milk to go on with?' asked Dotty solicitously.

'Half a pint of hogwash,' said Ella. 'I'll do.'

The two ladies collected their parcels, paid their bills to the less disdainful of the waitresses, and emerged into Lulling High Street.

'If them two wasn't ladies,' said one waitress to the other, 'they'd both be in the mad-house, and that's the honest truth.'

'You can say that again,' agreed her colleague, dusting a plate languidly against her lilac hip, as she watched the two customers disappearing into the distance.

St Andrew's church clock was striking six as Ella crossed the green to fetch the goat's milk.

In her basket lay a clean bottle, a copy of last week's *Punch* and a copy of *The Lady*. There was also a paper bag containing half a pound or so of early black plums from the ancient tree in Ella's garden.

The air was warm and soft. The gentle golden light of a fine September evening gilded the Cotswold stone buildings, and turned the windows of the church into sheets of dazzling flame.

Albert Piggott stood motionless in the church porch. With his head out-thrust and his drooping mouth he reminded Ella of a tortoise she had owned as a child.

'Lovely day!' she called.

'Swarmin' with gnats,' responded the sexton gloomily. 'Sign of rain.'

Ella did not pursue the conversation, but strode rapidly down the narrow alley beside the Piggotts' abode to the field path which led to Dotty's cottage some half a mile away.

As she approached the garden gate she became conscious of a voice – Dotty's voice – keeping up a relentless monologue.

'Come on, boys, out you come! Come and get your good suppers! It's no use skulking in there. How d'you expect to get anyone to give you a good home if you behave so foolishly? Be brave now. Show yourselves. No food for cowardly cats. Come out and feed properly, or back it goes into the house!'

Ella waited, out of sight, irresolute.

Dotty's slightly hectoring tone changed to one of maudlin encouragement. Obviously, one brave kitten had emerged from its hiding place.

'Sweet thing!' murmured Dotty. 'Brave puss! Now, don't run away again. There's a *good* little cat.'

There was a sound of lapping, and Ella approached cautiously. Her shadow fell across the dish of milk, the kitten vanished with a squawk, and Dotty gave a startled squeal of exasperation.

'There now, Ella, you've scared them! Just as they were coming out. What on earth brings you here at just this particularly awkward time?'

'Goat's milk,' said Ella mildly. 'And, dammit all, Dot, I had to come *some* time. How long do you spend here squatting on that uncomfortable log?'

'I try and have half an hour in the morning and another about this time,' replied Dotty, dusting her skirt sketchily. She peered through her steel-rimmed spectacles into the depths of the log shack, but nothing stirred. She sighed sadly.

'Well, that's ruined this evening's session. Come along, Ella, and fetch the milk.'

She led the way into the kitchen, and Ella thought, yet again, what a perfect film set it would make for a witch's background.

Bundles of drying herbs hung from the rafters. A dead chicken, waiting to be plucked, hung upside down against the back of the door. A pungent reek floated from a large copper preserving pan bubbling on the stove, and the kitchen table was crowded with jars, bottles, newspaper cuttings, an enormous ledger with mottled edges, and a butcher's cleaver still sticky with blood.

Add a few living touches, thought Ella, such as frogs and bats, and the place would be complete.

The milk, mercifully, was already bottled, corked, and standing on the cool brick floor in Dotty's larder.

'That looks fine,' said Ella warmly, surveying the beautiful rich colour admiringly. What were a few germs anyway? 'Makes my homogenized muck look pretty silly. Thank you very much, Dotty dear. And what do I owe you?'

'Say sixpence,' said Dotty vaguely.

'Make it a shilling,' replied Ella, slapping the coin down upon the laden table. 'Suits me, if it suits you.'

'Very well,' responded Dotty. 'I must admit the kittens are costing me quite a bit to feed. I'm having to buy tins of stuff called "Pretty-Puss" and "Katsluvit". I don't approve of the names, but the kittens seem to eat everything ravenously. Such a relief! It means that I can take the mother cat to the vet next week.'

'Got homes yet?' asked Ella.

'The Youngs are having one. Paul was persistent, I gather, sensible child. And Dimity is dithering. Frightened of the traffic, I think.'

'I'll speak to her,' said Ella ominously. 'Cats must take their chance these days.'

The two ladies made their farewells, one moving off to Thrush Green, and the other setting out yet again, to try her luck with the interrupted cat-taming in the log shed.

Dimity Henstock's dinner party was an outstanding success right from the start.

Betty Bell was in charge of the kitchen that evening. She was a first-class cook, even if her cleaning and dusting were sketchy, having been trained in a ducal establishment in the north, under a dragon of a cook who had terrified young Betty but had taught her supremely well.

To be able to engage Betty Bell for the evening was a sure

foundation for the success of a dinner party, as Thrush Green and Lulling hostesses knew well.

As Dimity looked at the seating arrangements in the dining-room, she could hear Betty singing cheerfully as she coped with leg of mutton, onion sauce, roast potatoes, cauliflower, peas and young Brussels sprouts. She had also made some attractive shrimp and grapefruit cocktails and set them in place, and insisted on adding a vast apple pie to the delicate orange mousse, which Dimity had made and privately thought quite adequate, for the sweet course.

'You wants more than that for men,' maintained Betty stoutly. 'No *body* to mousse. Men likes a bit of pastry.'

'There will be cheese and biscuits,' Dimity pointed out, 'if they are still hungry.'

'Not the same,' asserted Betty. 'Mrs Furze,' she added, referring to the she-dragon who had taught her all she knew, 'wouldn't dream of putting but the one sweet on the table.'

'Very well,' agreed Dimity. She knew when she was beaten. 'Certainly make an apple pie. I'm sure it will be delicious.'

The dinner table pleased even her over-anxious eye. She had polished the rector's silver candlesticks herself and the light of six candles fell upon the bowl of orange dahlias which formed the centrepiece. For once, the bleak lofty room looked warm and inviting. The carpet was thin and worn, the furniture shabby, but the kindly candlelight hid these things, and Dimity felt proud of her arrangements.

Dimity longed to furnish the rectory as she knew it should be furnished. It needed thick velvet curtains at the tall narrow windows to mitigate the draughts and the gauntness of design. It was a house which cried out for soft carpets and central heating, but there was no money for such luxuries on the rector's stipend, and Dimity loved him far too well to ask him for the impossible. The floors of the bedrooms and the long draughty passages were covered with the dark brown linoleum chosen by a predecessor of Charles Henstock's. It was badly worn, but gleamed with years of polishing. Nevertheless, it wrung Dimity's heart to see her beloved Charles walking barefoot on a winter's morning upon such an inhospitable surface. The few small rugs available lay like tiny rafts upon the glassy sea. Sometimes Dimity envied her husband his Spartan attitude to their surroundings, and there were times when she thought, with secret longing, of the small cosy bedroom under the thatched roof opposite, where she had slept snugly for so many years.

Eight people sat down to enjoy the leg of mutton. The guests were Edward and Joan Young, Doctor Lovell and his wife Ruth, Harold Shoosmith and the newcomer, Phil Prior.

Dimity had selected her visitors with considerable care. She wanted to introduce Mrs Prior to people much of her own age. The Lovells and Youngs were in their early thirties, but try as she might Dimity could find no unattached male of that age to balance her dinner table.

'What a *blessing* Harold is single,' she said to her husband whilst making her preparations. 'We could do with half a dozen more men really in Thrush Green. I mean, if one were going to have a really big affair it would be simple to find a dozen single women – Ella, Dotty, the three Lovelock sisters and so on – but where are the *men*?'

'Safely married,' replied Charles smugly. 'Like me. You can't have it both ways, my dear.'

'And even dear Harold is a little older than I really wanted,' mused Dimity to herself.

'He's no older than I am,' the rector pointed out mildly, and was amused to see the contrition on his wife's face as she strove to make amends.

In any case, thought Dimity, looking happily about her dinner table, Harold was easily the most handsome man there, and by far the best dressed. Why was it, she wondered, that young men these days appeared so scruffy compared with their elders? Their wives looked so pretty in their silk frocks; one sister in green and the other in striped grey and white, while the newcomer wore a softly-draped frock of very fine wool starred with tiny flowers. A Liberty print, guessed Dimity correctly, thinking how beautifully it set off the girl's dark looks.

She was more animated than Dimity had ever seen her. Among these old friends, so easy with each other, she showed no shyness.

'And how many committees do you find yourself on?' asked Harold.

'Why, none yet.'

'Amazing! I was on *five* before I'd been here a month,' said Harold. 'You see, your turn will come. Which reminds me, Charles, I haven't been able to type the minutes of the Entertainments Committee. My typewriter has collapsed.'

'What's the matter with it?' asked Mrs Prior with genuine interest.

'Asthma, I should imagine, from the rhythmic squeaks it gives out. It's gone in for an overhaul. Poor old thing, it's well over thirty years old and spent most of its life in the tropics, so it's not done too badly.'

'I could type the minutes, if you'd like me to,' offered the girl.

'Do you type too?' asked the rector, in open admiration. 'How clever of you! Without looking at the keys?'

'Of course,' she said, laughing. 'I should have been thrown out of my typing class pretty smartly if I'd dared to look at the keyboard.'

'Well, I've never been able to master a typewriter,' confessed the rector. 'I once tried to type "How doth the little crocodile" on Harold's machine, and it made an awful lot of 8s and half-pennies, I remember. Do you use yours much?'

'I do a column for a girls' weekly,' said Mrs Prior. 'About five hundred words. And a few book reviews.'

This modest disclosure brought forth a buzz of excited comment. Thrush Green had no writers among its inhabitants, and to meet someone who not only wrote, but who actually had those writings published was indeed thrilling.

'I've always thought I could write,' observed Edward Young, adding predictably, 'if I only had the time.'

'I couldn't,' said his brother-in-law honestly. 'It's quite bad enough writing prescriptions. Anything imaginative would floor me completely.'

'When you say "a column",' said Dimity, 'do you mean a short story?'

'A brief article,' answered the girl, 'on some topical matter which would interest girls. Sometimes I make one of the books the subject of the column – that's cheating, I feel, but the editor approves.'

'You must enjoy it.'

'Not always – but it's well paid, and the editor is a sweetie.'

'Mary has just learnt to hold a crayon properly,' said Ruth Lovell proudly, 'and has scribbled on *every page* of the laundry book.' The company agreed that this might, conceivably show literary promise.

The orange mousse and the apple pie were eaten to the exchange of news about children, and no more was said about the writing until the company were enjoying Dimity's excellent coffee by the drawing-room fire.

Harold Shoosmith, who settled himself next to the girl, asked if she would find it a nuisance to type the minutes.

'Or I could do them myself, if I might borrow the typewriter for half an hour,' he said. 'Whichever is simpler for you. They only take up a page of quarto-size.'

'Bring them in tomorrow,' said the girl. 'I shall be in all day.'

And so the matter was left, and the evening passed very pleasantly in general conversation, except for ten minutes of television news which Edward Young asked if he might see as he had heard that a house he had restored for a wealthy pop singer had just been burned out and it might be shown on the screen.

The company obligingly sat through a student demonstration, plentifully sprinkled with bleeding noses and blasphemies, a multiple car crash on a motorway from which a stretcher, ominously blanketed, was removed, an interview with a distracted mother whose child had been abducted, and the arrival at London airport of a half-naked film star whose long unkempt hair was something of a blessing in view of her neck-line. But Edward Young's burned-out masterpiece was not included among the attractions, and everyone was thankful when the set was switched off.

'I don't call that news, do you?' said Charles Henstock. 'Not by Thrush Green standards anyway. What I mean by news is hearing about Dotty Harmer's kittens, or Albert Piggott's prize onions or meeting a charming newcomer to the village,' he said, bowing slightly to his guest of honour.

'And why should one be subjected to all these horrors on one's own hearth rug?' agreed Doctor Lovell. 'To think we *pay* for it too! It's galling.'

'Too bad about your house,' said Dimity to Edward, 'it probably wasn't ghastly enough to compete with all that violence. I suppose nobody was burned?'

'No one, as far as I know.'

'That accounts for it,' said Dimity reasonably. 'An item of news like that, without so much as a few charred bones, or firemen falling screaming into the blaze, wouldn't stand a chance.'

At eleven o'clock the guests began to make their farewells. Only the Lovells drove home, for their house was a mile away. The rest of the guests lived round the green and walked across the grass together.

Already most of the houses were in darkness, for country people have to be up betimes and midnight is considered a very late hour indeed for going to bed.

But a light shone still at Tullivers, where Winnie Bailey sat sewing, her young charge fast asleep in the bedroom above. She heard his mother's light footsteps on the path, and put down her needlework.

'My word,' she said, looking at the girl's glowing face in the doorway, 'I can see you've had a lovely evening. And so, my dear, have I!'

7. *A Question of Divorce*

THE next morning Harold Shoosmith crossed the green to Tullivers.

He found Mrs Prior alone, her typewriter already on the table and an appetizing smell of steak and kidney casserole floating from the kitchen.

'Jeremy gets home at twelve,' she said, 'and we have our main meal then. It gets cooking over and done with for the day, and I boil an egg or have some cheese and biscuits when Jeremy's in bed.'

'I do much the same,' said Harold, 'though Betty Bell is always willing to come and fatten me up, if given half a chance.'

He put the hand-written minutes on the table.

'Are you sure it's not an imposition?' he asked.

The girl laughed.

'It will be a change from the perils-of-Pauline stuff I'm attempting at the moment. I'm trying to sell some short stories to magazines.'

'Here, or overseas?'

'Here, and in America. They pay most generously over there, but I doubt if my stuff will be suitable.'

Harold Shoosmith gazed thoughtfully through the window.

'I've an editor friend in one of these magazine combines. If I could be of any help—?'

'You're very kind. If I get too many rejections, I'll remember. I'm sorting out old material just now, and trying to bring it up-to-date.'

'Wouldn't it be better to start again?'

'I need some money pretty quickly,' replied the girl frankly. 'This house – as always – has cost far more to put to rights than I bargained for, and if I can sell some stories now, I can get down to some really new stuff while they are being considered. Editors seem to take an unconscionable length of time to make up their minds.'

'If you think I could help by looking through any of your stories to see if they seem to be on the right lines for Frank, I would be only too happy to do so,' said Harold.

'I might be very glad indeed,' replied Phil, 'but let's see how my luck turns out in the next few weeks. In any case I've always got my column to keep the wolf from the door.'

'Yes, indeed,' said Harold, but there was doubt in his tone.

'And my husband is very generous,' the girl added, a shade too swiftly. 'But, of course, one likes to feel independent.'

'Of course,' echoed Harold, obviously bemused, but doing his best to cope with the situation. There was a slight pause. The clock struck eleven, and brought Harold to his senses.

'Well, I must be off. When shall I call for the minutes?'

'Oh, don't bother. I'll pop over after tea, if I may.'

'That would be very kind of you,' said Harold gravely, making for the door.

He crossed the green thoughtfully.

'That devil's left her!' he said to a startled blackbird on his gatepost.

Harold Shoosmith had guessed correctly, but it was Winnie Bailey who heard the truth first from the girl herself.

It was a fine October afternoon, clear and vivid, and Winnie noticed how auburn the chestnut avenue had become since the first few frosts. Her spirits were high as she breathed the keen air.

It was quite two weeks, she told herself, since she had talked to Phil, but this was not surprising. One's next-door neighbours, however dear, tend to be neglected for the plain reason that they *are* next-door. It is the friends at a distance whom one makes the effort to meet. But she had caught a glimpse of her at the typewriter, and knew that she was busy.

She was calling now to see if she could persuade her to collect for Poppy Day. The Misses Lovelace who had quartered Lulling and Thrush Green between them for decades, had decided that their arthritis and general frailty would not allow them to continue the good work. To find one noble soul willing to turn out in November to rattle a collecting tin, is hard enough. To find *three* was proving a headache.

Full of hope, Winnie knocked with the late admiral's great brass dolphin on Tullivers' front door. It was opened by Phil herself, white of face and red of eye. Winnie Bailey, used as a doctor's wife to seeing men and women in misery, thought she had never seen quite such a tragic face.

'Phil, tell me!' she said impulsively, and then checked herself. 'No, my dear, let me creep away. You won't want to be bothered with callers just now.'

'Do *please* come in,' cried the girl. 'I need a friend badly.'

She led the way into the little sitting-room and motioned the older woman to take a seat. Winnie watched her as she put two logs on the dying fire. Her hands were trembling and tears were running unheeded down her cheeks.

'What is it?' begged Winnie. 'Someone ill? Or worse?'

'Worse,' choked the girl. 'It's my husband.'

'Not dead!' Winnie whispered.

'Oh no, thank God!' She gave a high, cracked laugh, frightening to hear. 'Though why I should thank God, I don't know. He's left me.'

'You poor dear,' said Winnie, patting the arm that was near her. She felt the gnawing pity and the tragic impotence which captures those who are in the presence of grief which they are powerless to assuage.

The girl fumbled for a damp handkerchief, mopped her eyes, and took a deep shuddering breath.

'He left me almost six months ago. Another woman, of course. A French woman – a buyer for one of the Paris houses. I met her once.'

She stopped, and mopped her eyes again.

'Perhaps it's just an infatuation,' said Winnie. 'Is she very attractive?'

'Not a bit,' cried Phil. She smiled damply. 'Well, I know I'm biased, but I don't think anyone – except John – would find her attractive. She's one of those bony Frenchwomen with a long face like a disapproving horse. Marvellous figure, of course, and dresses superbly, but no glamour-girl, I assure you.

'When he wrote and said that they were in love, I laughed out loud. It seemed so ludicrous, I just couldn't believe it – like some awful unspeakable joke.'

She helped herself to a cigarette, and lit it shakily.

'But it was no joke, as you can imagine. He came back several times to the flat, and was more determined each time to break with me. I tried desperately to keep my head. I was sure he would get tired of her – that it was, as you said, an infatuation. But the day came when he told me flatly that he was going to bring her to live in our house, and I must get out.

'Then I really did grovel! I told him I loved him still. I pleaded for Jeremy's sake. I swore I'd never throw this affair in his face if he'd think again. All useless!'

She stood up and walked restlessly about the little room.

'When I saw it was hopeless, and that she'd won, we made a scratch agreement to part. He gives me a regular amount each month, and he let me take the things I wanted from the Chelsea flat. But I absolutely refuse to give him a divorce. I still hope that he will come to his senses – or she will. Meanwhile, I try to keep it all from Jeremy. He adores John. It turns the knife pretty keenly, as you can imagine, when he prattles on about Daddy.'

She rolled the damp handkerchief into a ball and thrust it into her cardigan pocket.

'But this morning I had another letter. It's so terrible – so terrible—' She shook her head desperately, and a tear flew into the fire and sizzled.

'It's brought it home to me. We simply can't go on like this. I think I must make up my mind to go forward with a divorce. I suppose I've been evading it really – hoping, just stupidly hoping. The very idea of solicitors and courts and settlements and all the other beastly details absolutely revolts me. But I see now I must face it. He's only too pleased to give me grounds,' she added bitterly.

She sat down beside Winnie on the couch and took her hand.

'What would you do? What would you do if you were wretched me?'

Winnie put a comforting arm round the girl's shoulders.

'I should wait until tomorrow before doing anything. You've been brave and patient for so long, keep it up for a little longer. By that time it won't hurt so much and you'll tackle things better.'

The girl nodded dumbly.

'Don't write,' cautioned Winnie, 'don't telephone, don't talk to anyone about it until you've slept on it. No one will learn anything from me, I promise you. Then why not talk it over with your parents?'

'They died some years ago. I was an only child.'

'Is there someone else? A cousin, say, or a family friend?'

'Not that I could discuss this with. I would sooner tell our old family solicitor. He's wise and kind . . . a real friend.'

'Then why not go to him?'

'I'll do that,' whispered Phil huskily. 'It's keeping up appearances before Jeremy which is so hard. I've cried all day. Thank God he didn't seem to notice much at dinner time.'

'Let me walk across to the school when the children finish,' said Winnie, 'and take him back with me to tea.'

'No, really – '

'Please. I should love it, and it will give you a chance to get over the shock a little. I'll bring him back before half past six.'

She stood up and kissed the girl's pale cheek gently.

'Go and have a warm bath,' she advised. 'Hot water truly is the benison that Rupert Brooke said it was. And then give yourself a tot of something strong. You'll feel twice the girl.'

'You are an angel,' cried Phil, accompanying her to the door. 'I've done nothing but moan; and I haven't given you a chance to tell me what brings you here.'

Silently, Winnie held up the poppy tin.

'Of course I'll do it,' said Phil warmly. 'I can't weep for ever.'

Winnie's nephew Richard arrived the following week. He seemed genuinely grateful for his aunt's hospitality, and set himself out to be exceptionally charming to Doctor Bailey.

To Winnie's eye he looked very fit and lively, having acquired a fine tan in America which set off his pale hair and blue eyes. But it was not long before symptoms of the hypochondria which had always been present showed themselves in strength.

Two small bottles of pills stood by his plate at the first evening meal, and naturally excited the professional interest of his uncle.

'I find them indispensable,' said Richard. 'Otto – Professor Otto Goldstein, you know, the dietician – prescribed them for me. The red ones take care of the cholesterol, and these yellow and black torpedoes check acidity and act as a mild purge. Constipation is a terrible enemy.'

'You need a few prunes,' said the doctor, 'and a bit of rough-age.'

'Donald!' protested Winnie. 'Must you? At table?'

'Sorry, my dear, sorry,' said her husband.

'Too bad of me,' apologized Richard. 'Living alone such a lot makes one over-interested perhaps in one's natural functions.'

Winnie felt that this could lead to somewhat alarming disclosures which might be regretted by all. She changed the subject abruptly.

'You must meet our new neighbour,' she said brightly, passing her nephew Brussels sprouts. He held up a stern denying hand.

'Not for me, Aunt Winnie. Not *cooked* greens, I fear. Quite forbidden by Otto because of the gases. You haven't two or three raw ones, by any chance?'

'Not washed,' replied Winnie shortly, passing the rejected dish to her husband. She was keenly aware of the smile which hovered round the old doctor's lips.

'A pity,' murmured Richard, tackling pork chops *en casserole* with faint distaste.

'She plays bridge and whist, and is a very nice person to talk to. She writes.'

'Really?' replied Richard vaguely. Clearly his mind was concerned with his digestive tract.

'Will you have any spare evenings?' pursued Winnie.

Richard gave a gusty sigh, the sigh of one who, over-burdened with work, still enjoys his martyrdom.

'I very much doubt it. I shall be writing the notes on my experiments, of course, and I intend to spend as much time as I can refuting Carslake's idiotic principles. An obstinate fellow, if ever there was one, and a very elusive one too. I must thrash things out with him during the next few months.'

Winnie felt a wave of pity for the absent Professor Carslake. Richard, on the rampage, must be an appalling bore. She decided to put aside the idea of arranging Richard's social life at Thrush Green. Richard obviously did not want it, and was it really fair to her friends to inflict her nephew on them, she added reasonably to herself?

She watched him swallow a red pill and then a yellow and black one. It was quite apparent that he enjoyed them far more than the excellent dinner which Winnie had spent hours in preparing.

'Coffee?' she asked, rising from the table. 'Or does Professor Goldstein forbid that too?' There was an edge to her tone which did not escape her observant husband.

'No, indeed,' replied Richard, opening the drawing-room door politely. 'He approves of coffee, provided that the berries are really ripe, well roasted and coarsely ground. He doesn't agree with percolators, though. He always strains his through muslin. Do you?'

'Not with Nescafé,' said his aunt, with a hint of triumph, leading the way.

Richard was not the only one at Thrush Green suffering from indigestion. Doctor Lovell gave Albert Piggott a prescription, and then a few words of sound advice.

'Your wife's a fine cook, I know. But have small helpings. Don't forget your stomach was on short commons for years. It can't cope suddenly with all this bounty.'

Nelly tossed her head when Albert relayed this piece of advice.

'Good food never hurt nobody. Who does he think he is – the old Tin-ribs? He could do with a bit of flesh if anyone could. I bet he never gets his teeth into a decent steak-and-kidney pudding with that dreamy wife of his to do for him! Take them dratted pills, if you must, Albert Piggott, but you eat what's put in front of you and be thankful!'

She seemed to surpass herself in the days that followed. Cold fat bacon with pickled onions, fried cod cutlets with chips and peas, ox-tail soup, hot and glutinous, with swedes mashed with butter, all followed each other in succession, flaunting their richness and tempting Albert to fatal indulgences. His liverishness grew: his temper became more morose than ever. Nelly became aggrieved and nagged more and more bitterly.

The oilman began to figure largely in her conversation.

Albert, belching prettily after consuming a plate piled with pickled brawn, beetroot and bubble-and-squeak, spoke his mind.

'Can't you shut up about that ruddy oilman? Any more of it, and I'll tell 'im to stop calling. Givin' 'im cupsertea! Giggling like some fool-girl! I seen you at it – eggin' 'im on!'

'I'll thank you,' said Nelly haughtily, 'to mind your tongue. I only treat him civil. The poor chap's wife's left him.'

'Best day's work she ever done, I shouldn't wonder. You'd best take a leaf outer her book, my gal.'

'It's a pity if I can't have a friendly word with a gentleman without you getting filthy ideas into your head,' snapped Nelly, crashing cutlery about dangerously. 'The Lord alone knows I get little enough pleasure from your company. If you're not down the coke-hole you're in "The Two Pheasants". Why I was ever fool enough to give in to your begging of me to marry you I *cannot think*!'

This complete travesty of the facts of Albert's wooing rendered him speechless. But not for long.

'I *could say*,' said Albert, with a hiccup which marred the heavy solemnity of his utterance, 'exactly the same words, my gal, and with a deal more truth.'

Rumbling dangerously, he left his kitchen for something to settle his stomach next door.

8. *Gossip and Gardening*

THE rapid spread of news through a village is a natural phenomenon which is hard to explain. Phil Prior, after much inward wrestling, sought the advice of a London solicitor as a preliminary step to divorce from her husband.

She said not a word to anyone. Winnie Bailey, true to her promise, breathed not a syllable, not even to her husband. And yet the possibility of a divorce was generally known in Thrush Green.

How did such knowledge get around so swiftly? Winnie Bailey asked herself this, not for the first time. She supposed that someone originally made a shrewd guess, and passed on the surmise to a friend.

The friend then might say: 'I hear that there's talk of a divorce between the Priors.' And the next step would be: 'Have you heard about the Priors' divorce?' After that it was, of course, an accepted fact, despite the usual riders: 'Mind you, it's only what I've *heard*,' or 'It may be only idle gossip,' or 'Don't repeat it unless you hear it confirmed.' And, sure enough the snippet *would* be confirmed within an hour or so. Thus easily does bush-telegraph work in a small community.

Fortunately, Phil Prior, new to country ways, was not conscious of her matrimonial affairs being common gossip. Now that the first wretched step was taken, she felt calmer, and renewed her writing efforts.

Harold Shoosmith proved a wise adviser in literary matters, and the girl frequently called on him to discuss possible markets. Frank, the editor friend, had received one of her stories with guarded enthusiasm, but after keeping it for some time, returned it with the excuse that it 'was not strong enough' but said he would consider it again if she felt she could amend it.

'What does he mean exactly?' asked Phil of Harold Shoosmith. 'Not enough shooting and rape, do you think? I mean, I simply can't write about violence. The only person I ever saw shot, was a neighbour who was peppered in his garden by the boy next door with an air gun. To make matters worse, the wretched boy's feeble excuse was that he thought he was a squirrel! He weighed eighteen stone,' added Phil reminiscently.

'Insult to injury,' agreed Harold. 'I hope the boy had a good hiding on the spot, and was not made the subject of psychiatric reports two months later, when everyone had forgotten all about it.'

'Lord, yes!' cried Phil. 'This was years ago before such refinements were thought of. He was a good friend of mine, and he said he had one beating from his father and was then handed over to the victim of his attack. He didn't seem to bear any grudge about it. He was always a resilient child.'

She turned again to her typescript.

'But how on earth can I make it *stronger*? I wish editors would either reject a thing outright, or take it as it is. I do loathe messing about with a piece of writing which, after all, you have made as near perfect in the first place as you possibly can.'

'I'd be inclined to send him another,' advised Harold, 'while the going's good, and mull over this one for a bit. Tell him you will let him have it later, when you've had a chance to revise it.'

He watched the girl turning the pages, a worried frown creasing her brow. Damn Frank, he thought suddenly! And that wretched husband too! Why should such a nice woman have all this confounded work and worry? She should be enjoying life, not fighting for existence.

'Come and see my last few roses,' he said, rising abruptly. Suddenly, he longed for fresh air and sunshine.

Harold's garden was quite six times the size of Tullivers' but was in a state of exquisite neatness.

'With no help at all?' queried the girl unbelievingly, gazing about her.

'Piggott comes for an hour or so when he needs a little extra drinking money,' said Harold. 'But I find I can keep it fairly trim now that it's in order.'

He snipped another rose to add to the bouquet he was making.

'I wish you would let me help you with your garden,' he

continued. 'It would be such a pleasure to me, and if it is straightened up this autumn it should be so much easier to manage next year. As you see, I'm well ahead here, and could easily spare the time, if you would allow me to trespass.'

'You are very, very kind,' said Phil warmly, accepting the bouquet gratefully. 'And these are simply lovely. To be honest, I'd be terribly thankful for a hand with some bramble bushes which seem to have roots from here to Lulling.'

'I'll be over tomorrow afternoon, if that suits you,' said Harold briskly.

They walked together to the gate, and Harold watched her cross the green, the bunch of late roses making a splash of colour against her pale coat.

Another figure was advancing, in the distance, from his right. It was Dotty Harmer, struggling with a large cat basket. Heavy though it appeared to be, Dotty was making good headway, so that Harold, who felt unequal to Dotty's conversation at the moment, retreated strategically to the peace of his study, chiding himself for cowardice and lack of chivalry the while.

Dotty was bound for the Young's house, a bewildered ginger kitten mewing its protests as they made the uphill journey together.

She was glad to rest the basket on the doorstep as she rang the bell. The kitten, relieved that the motion had stopped, now sat mute among its blankets, but watched warily.

Paul opened the door, and fell upon his knees in front of the basket adoringly.

'You nice little puss! Are you coming to live here, then? Dear little cat, nice little – '

At this point, Dotty poked him sharply, bringing his ecstasies to an abrupt halt.

'Where are your manners, boy? What about speaking to me before you fuss with the cat!'

Scarlet with shame, Paul struggled to his feet and made apologies, just as his mother arrived.

'Please come in; I'd no idea you were going to bring the

kitten. We intended to come and fetch it to save you trouble.'

'No bother,' said Dotty, about to lift the basket again.

'Let Paul do it,' said Joan. 'It really is very sweet of you to have carried it all the way here. What a very pretty one!'

They stood and admired the minute scrap, crouching among its bedding.

'Now, if I were you,' said Dotty, taking charge, 'I should put the basket in an empty warm room, and put its earth box and a saucer of milk there too. Then make sure it cannot get out of the room, open the door of the basket, and let it explore for some hours.'

'What about buttering its paws?' asked Paul, anxious to show his knowledge.

'Fiddlesticks!' snapped Dotty. 'You do as I say, and he'll soon settle down.'

'Do you think it is a he?' asked Joan, with some anxiety.

'That I can't be sure of. Cats are very difficult to sort out. But the vet will cope at six months either way.'

'But I should *like* it to have kittens!' protested Paul. He was on his knees again, one finger stroking the kitten's head through the wire door of the basket.

'Precocious, that child!' said Dotty to his mother, in a dark aside. 'Who said anything about kittens, young man?' she added forthrightly. 'We know what we're about, and what's best for that cat. Just you go and do as I said.'

'Take it up to the spare bedroom,' directed his mother, 'and I'll come up in a moment. Don't undo the door until I come.'

Paul picked up the basket. Without being prompted, he smiled upon Dotty and spoke his thanks.

'That's more like it,' said Dotty grudgingly. 'Remembered your manners after all! Now, take care of that mite. It's the tamest of the litter. It wants plenty of love, warmth and food, in that order. And if I hear you've tormented it *in any way*, I shall *take it back*!'

'Yes, Miss Harmer,' said Paul meekly, and began to mount the stairs with his treasure.

'Not a bad child,' conceded Dotty, watching his departing back.

'We find him fairly satisfactory,' agreed Joan drily. The mild irony was lost upon her guest.

'It's because you haven't kept many animals,' said Dotty. 'Now, they are *completely* satisfactory. Which reminds me, I must return to mine. I've left a saucepan of fish simmering, and I don't want it to boil dry.'

'Nothing worse,' said Joan, 'than the smell of boiling fish, I agree.'

'It's not the smell I worry about,' cried Dotty, stepping out of the front door, 'but the dear cats won't touch fish if it's the slightest bit caught.'

She set off at a fast trot towards the pathway to Lulling Woods and her animal family.

True to his word, Harold Shoosmith made his way to Tullivers the next afternoon. The girl came to the door immediately, for she had seen him pass the window. Papers were spread upon the table, and her typewriter stood among the litter.

'Don't let me stop you,' said Harold. 'I think I know where the brambles are.'

He pointed to the wall which divided Tullivers' garden from the Baileys' orchard. A border lay at its foot, but was so overgrown with many weeds, including the brambles, that it was practically invisible.

'There are some tools in the shed at the back of the house,' said Phil. 'I'll get them for you.'

'No, no! I can find them,' said Harold. 'Don't let me interrupt the writing.'

He made his way round the house as the girl returned to her typing.

He found the shed easily enough, but surveyed the tools with mingled dismay and pity. There were very few of them, and all looked hopelessly inadequate or outworn to Harold's sharp eye.

The only fork available was a very large, heavy old veteran with wide flat tines, meant for digging up potatoes. The spade was equally heavy, and coated with dried Cotswold clay. The handle was badly cracked and had been bound, in an amateurish fashion, with string. Two trowels, a rake with a wobbly head, a birch broom, and a rusty bill-hook comprised the rest of the gardening equipment, except for a lawn-mower whose newness simply threw the age of the other tools into sharp relief.

Very quietly, Harold went round the back of the house to the gate, so that he did not need to pass the worker's window, and went to collect his own shining equipment from across the green.

Half an hour with a swinging mattock loosened the worst of the roots, and Harold enjoyed piling up the rubbish on the ashy remains of earlier bonfires. Brambles, elder shoots, and lofty nettles removed, it was possible to see the remains of the border. Among the shorter weeds which clothed the earth, Harold found clumps of irises, peonies and pinks still surviving suffocation. At one time the border had been well-stocked. It would be very rewarding, thought Harold, to see it trim and colourful again.

With his light fork he loosened wild strawberry runners, groundsel, docks, chickweed and yards and yards of matted couch grass roots.

The pile of rubbish grew higher and higher, and Harold was just contemplating the possibility of lighting a bonfire, as he straightened his back, when Phil came out from the house to admire his handiwork.

'And I believe you've got some nerines among those clumps of bulbs,' said Harold enthusiastically. 'It's an ideal spot for them there. Don't disturb them. I'll put a marker by them next time I come.'

'But you can't spend too much time among my weeds,' protested Phil. 'Your own will sneak up on you.'

Harold, flushed with his exertions, looked contentedly at the first few yards of border revealed.

'I'd like to finish this job,' he said. 'Three or four afternoons should see it cleared.'

Phil was looking at his fork with envy.

'Is it stainless steel?'

He said, somewhat apologetically, that it was.

'One gets used to one's own tools, you know. When you

replace, my dear, I do advise you to get stainless steel. It is well worth it.'

'I shan't be replacing for some time,' said Phil, laughing. 'But I came to tell you that I had made some tea.'

It was snug in the little house. Harold had been so happy and busy in the garden that he had not noticed the grey clouds scudding ominously from the west. A spatter of rain on the window heralded a wet evening.

Phil nodded at a large envelope, stamped, sealed and ready for the post.

'I've taken your advice,' she said, 'and looked out another story. I do hope he likes this one. I'm going to alter the one he's just sent back. I had a brain-wave last night in bed which might work, I think.'

'Any more luck?'

'A hopeful letter from a women's magazine in America. I sent an article about how to encourage children to take to books. So many don't, you know. Thank heaven Jeremy likes reading!'

'I must be off,' said Harold, rising. 'Thank you for restoring me with tea. I'll be in London for the next two days, but I hope you'll let me tackle the border when I come back.'

'You know I shall be very, very grateful,' Phil replied, opening the front door.

The rain fell heavily, splashing from the admiral's brass dolphin upon the door mat.

Harold picked up his bundle of tools, neatly swathed in a sack.

'Here, give me your letters,' he said, eyeing the downpour. 'I'll put them in the box as I pass. You'll get drenched if you go out, and Willie's due to collect any minute now.'

She put the bundle of letters, including the large packet, into his outstretched hand.

'You really should spit on the big one, for luck,' she called after him as he hurried down the path.

With his tools across his shoulder and the letters in his hand, Harold made his way to the letter box at the corner of Thrush Green. The Cotswold stone glistened with rain around the red oblong.

Harold inserted the small letters, and then carefully threaded the large one into the aperture. It fell with a satisfying plop, and as it vanished Harold wished it luck.

Whistling cheerfully, he splashed beneath the chestnuts to his home, thinking gaily of work well done and the pleasure derived from a good-looking woman's company.

Little did he think that the packet he had so carefully posted would be the cause of much concern for the pair of them.

On that same rainy evening Sam Curdle, who had managed to conduct his affairs in a relatively honest manner for some months, succumbed to temptation.

It so happened that Percy Hodge, the farmer in whose yard the battered Curdle caravan was housed, had seen some fine wallflower plants going cheaply in Lulling market. He bought twelve dozen and left the twelve newspaper-shrouded bundles lodged against the corner of his back porch.

'If you get that lot put in for me tomorrow, Sam,' he told him, 'there's half a sack of spuds for you. Fill up the round bed in the front of the house, and the border under the greenhouse. You'll need the gross, I reckon, to make a tidy show.'

Sam agreed with alacrity. Half a sack of potatoes would be most welcome to the family, and planting out a few wallflowers was easy work.

It took Sam less than five minutes to plan how he could make a few shillings for himself on the deal. Percy Hodge would be out all day at a sheep sale, Sam knew. By planting the wallflowers carefully, he reckoned he could keep two, or possibly three, dozen aside for sale elsewhere.

That new woman at Tullivers, he pondered, as he lay beside his snoring Bella that night. She looked the sort who might fall for a few plants, and Lord alone knew that garden of hers was in need of something. Sam surmised, correctly, that she would know little about prices, and would not be the type to haggle.

What should he ask now? Six shillings a dozen? Too steep, perhaps, even for a greenhorn such as that Londoner. He'd heard down at 'The Two Pheasants' that most of the locals were getting twopence a plant. Maybe it would be best to settle for fivepence. After all, he reasoned happily to himself, if he swiped two dozen from Percy Hodge he'd make a clear ten bob. With any luck, though, he could appropriate three dozen. Fifteen bob, now that really would be useful! He might even have a flutter on a horse in the afternoon, and make a bit that way too.

As for Percy Hodge, he'd never notice a few wallflowers missing once the beds were planted. It was a chance too good to miss, Sam told himself.

Well content with his plans, he turned on his side, wrenched rather more of his share of the marital blankets from his wife's recumbent form, and settled to sleep.

9. Sam Curdle Tries His Tricks

On the whole, Winnie Bailey found Richard's stay with them less punishing than she had first feared. Nevertheless, she was becoming heartily sick of his preoccupation with his alimentary canal, and said as much to her husband one day when her nephew was safely in Oxford about his affairs.

'Ignore it,' advised Dr Bailey.

'That's easier said than done,' said Winnie, knitting briskly. 'After all, I have to spend a great deal of time and thought on our meals, and it really is maddening to see him picking about like an old hen.'

'The boy wants more exercise,' said her husband. 'As far as I can see, the walk from the front door to the garage is about the sum total of his exertions. He's bound to be liverish.'

'Have a word with him,' begged Winnie. 'It really can't be good for him to be so introspective about his food, and honestly, it's driving me quite crazy.'

'I'll do my best,' promised her husband, but privately he had little hope of curing a hypochondriac so easily.

His chance came a day or two later when Winnie was out at an evening meeting of the Lulling Field Club, accompanied by her old friend Dotty Harmer. Winnie had left cold chicken and ham, and a fresh green salad for the menfolk, with a delicious orange trifle for their pudding. She herself would be dining on two Marie biscuits and a cup of weak tea, as the Lulling meeting began at 7.00 p.m. and these exciting refreshments would be served at half-time – somewhere about 8.15 p.m. This was the usual pattern of evening meetings in Lulling and Thrush Green, and accounted for the internal rumblings of hungry stomachs which invariably accompanied local lectures and whist drives.

Dr Bailey helped his nephew to the meat which his wife had left neatly sliced on the dish.

'Oh, far less than that, please,' begged Richard. 'Somehow I seem to be averse to flesh these days.'

The doctor obligingly transferred two small slices to his own plate.

He watched Richard turning over the salad. Now that Winnie had made him aware of the young man's foibles, he noticed how anxiously he picked over the greenery, selecting a lettuce leaf here, a sprig or two of cress there and taking care to miss the sliced cucumber which hid among the leaves.

'Averse to cucumber too?' asked the older man pleasantly. 'I always enjoy cucumber, I must confess.' He helped himself generously.

'Aunt Winnie's food is always delicious, but I don't seem to get as hungry as I used to do. And then, of course, I like to keep to Otto's diet. I'm sure he's in advance of his time in these matters.'

'You need more exercise,' said the doctor.

'I agree, my dear uncle. I couldn't agree more. As you know, I've had to cut down my walking time since I've been engaged on this Oxford project, and I certainly feel all the worse for it,' replied Richard vigorously. 'It's one of the reasons why I try to cut down on my intake of food.'

'You probably worry too much about your work at the moment. Nothing like worry to deaden the appetite. You should take life more easily.'

Richard, chewing his lettuce as conscientiously as Mr Gladstone, looked gratified. Rarely did he get any active encouragement to talk about his health. To have the attention of a medical man, even a medical man with ideas as antiquated as his uncle's, was wholly delightful. He became more confidential, encouraged not only by the doctor's interest but also by the absence of his aunt.

'I think you are quite right, uncle. Otto seemed to think that I was a shade too highly-strung. He suggested that marriage might help. It relieves tension, you know.'

'It can increase it,' observed the doctor drily, dabbing his lips with his napkin. 'A lot depends on one's wife.'

'I have been thinking about it,' continued Richard, brushing aside his uncle's comment. 'It looks as though I shall need to settle in London within the next year or so, and it would be wise, I think, to buy a small house. A wife would be very useful domestically. I'm no hand at cleaning and cooking, I'm afraid.'

'You could always get a housekeeper,' said Dr Bailey, with a touch of asperity.

'I was thinking of Otto's advice. He seemed to think that I needed a comfortable settled background in order to do my best work. And although I don't consciously miss it, busy as I am with my research, he assures me that I am deeply deprived sexually.'

'You could always get a mistress too,' said Dr Bailey, even more frostily. His thin fingers drummed on the edge of the table. Winnie would have known that he was becoming very angry indeed. Richard blundered on.

'I dislike the idea,' he said primly. 'And frankly, uncle, I'm surprised that you suggest it. No, I feel sure that I'm ready for marriage. After all, I shall be thirty-three next birthday. I think it's time I found a wife.'

'You may have some difficulty,' said Dr Bailey.

'Really?' Richard was genuinely surprised. 'I don't want to appear conceited, but I'm reasonably healthy and good-looking, and as for prospects – well, I think I can safely say that I shall be at the top of my particular tree within the next five years.'

The older man hit the table so sharply that the glasses jumped.

'Richard, will you never grow up?'

His nephew looked at him with startled blue eyes.

'You seem to view marriage purely as a panacea for your own ills,' continued the doctor, his cheeks flushed with exasperation. 'You talk as though a wife were a cross between a box of tranquillizing pills and a Hoover. *Not once* have you mentioned affection, respect or mutual happiness. D'you think any girl worth her salt is going to take you on, on your terms? Believe me, Richard, you're the one that will remain single if all you are offering are the attractions you've just mentioned.'

'Uncle—' began Richard, in protest but he was ignored.

'I must say it, my boy, hard though it sounds. You are as bone-selfish now as you were at seven years' old, and you've grown no wiser with the years. Marriage might well do you a power of good – heaven knows you need humanizing somehow – but I pity the girl who ever takes you on.'

The doctor raised his glass and sipped some water. Across the table his nephew sat transfixed, a slightly sulky look replacing the one of utter surprise.

'I'm sorry I should have upset you,' he said stiffly at last. 'I had no idea I was so objectionable.'

'Oh, tut-tut!' said Dr Bailey testily. 'Don't get in a huff over a bit of straight talking. You've got your good points, my boy, as we all have – but unselfishness is not among them at the moment. You think over what I've said now.'

He reached for the trifle.

'Let me give you a helping of this, Richard. Dr Goldstein would approve, I feel sure.'

But Richard was not to be mollified by a helping of trifle or a quip about his medical adviser. He rose from the table, his whole demeanour expressing acutely wounded dignity.

'No, thank you, uncle. My appetite has completely vanished after those remarks. If you'll excuse me, I will go for a walk.'

'You couldn't do better,' said the doctor cheerfully. 'And take an alka-seltzer before you go to bed. You'll be as right as a trivet in the morning.'

When Winnie returned, Richard was still out.

'Walking somewhere,' said her husband, in answer to her inquiries. 'Getting over the sulks. We had that little talk you suggested.'

'Oh, Donald, you haven't upset him, have you?'

'I rather hope so. We went from food to marriage. Richard seems to think that a wife might be a useful cure for his constipation and save him from doing his own chores.'

'Donald! Is that all?'

'That's what I asked him. He's out now, I fancy, trying to find the answer.'

Next door, at Tullivers, Harold Shoosmith continued his

assault on the neglected border. Some days had elapsed since his first visit, and on his second he was surprised to see that the narrow bed under the dining-room window had been planted with healthy wallflower plants.

'Your handiwork?' he asked.

'Yes. Are they put in properly? Not too close, are they?'

'No, they're just right. Very fine specimens too. They put my own to shame. Where did you buy them?'

'As a matter of fact,' said Phil, 'a sandy-haired man came to the door with them while you were in London. I can't remember his name – but he's often about. He helps old Piggott sometimes, I think.'

'Sam Curdle,' said Harold grimly.

Phil looked at him anxiously.

'Why, what's wrong?'

'What did he ask for them?'

'I paid him ten shillings for two dozen. Was that too much?'

'Much too much, my dear. Especially as he probably pinched them in the first place.'

'Damn!' said Phil softly, thrusting her hands into her coat pockets and surveying the border ruefully. 'I might have known. What shall I do? If these have been lifted from someone else's garden, they'll be furious.'

'Leave it to me,' replied Harold. 'I'll have a word with Sam Curdle. He's no business to charge more than two shillings a dozen anyway, and well he knows it. Don't have any dealing with that chap. You'll be done every time.'

'I'll watch him in future,' promised Phil. 'How I do hate to be fooled!'

'Who doesn't?' smiled Harold, moving off to his digging.

Sam Curdle's peccadillo, as it happened, had already been discovered. Percy Hodge had a farmer's sharp eye, and a pretty shrewd idea of how twelve dozen plants would look in the garden beds allotted to Sam's care. It did not take him long to discover that they were fairly sparsely planted. He confronted Sam the morning after the sheep sale.

Sam denied the charge.

'You be allus down on us Curdles,' he complained, a gypsy

whine creeping into his voice. 'Every blessed plant as was outside your back door I planted, as God's my Saviour.'

'Fat lot of saving you'll get,' said Percy Hodge roundly.
'There's a good score or more plants missing, and I want them
back. Understand?'

'How'm I to get 'em? I tell you, sir, they're all set in, as you
can see.'

'You get them back, Curdle, or tell me what's happened to
'em. You can take yourself and your missus off my land if I
don't get the rights of this business. You had fair warning when
I let you come into the yard.'

'You be a hard man,' whimpered Sam. In truth, he was
more frightened of his wife's reaction to the news than his
master's threats. Bella could be ferocious in anger, and Sam
still bore the scars of marital battle from earlier engagements
with his wife.

At that moment, the telephone rang and Percy Hodge strode
indoors to answer it, leaving Sam to his thoughts.

For the rest of that day, and the next, Sam puzzled over his
problem. Not for a minute did he consider telling the truth.
Such a straightforward course was completely foreign to Sam's
devious temperament. Somehow he must slide out of this tangle
of trouble and, more important still, without Bella finding
out.

Fate was against him. Percy Hodge and Harold Shoosmith
met on the evening of Harold's discovery at Tullivers. Both
men were on their way to the post-box at the corner of Thrush
Green. After the usual greetings, and comment on the weather,
Harold came to the point.

'Is Sam Curdle still with you?'

'Yes, indeed, the rogue. But he'll not be with me much
longer, I fancy. He's up to his old tricks. Pinching wallflower
plants this time.'

'I'll show you where they are,' said Harold, and led the way
across the road to Tullivers.

It was beginning to get dark, but the sturdy plants, so
carefully put in by Phil, were clearly to be seen. The two men
gazed at them over the gate.

'D'you know what he got for them?' asked Percy, turning away. The two men moved towards the green.

'He fleeced Mrs Prior of ten shillings,' said Harold. 'It's despicable.'

'She must be a green 'un,' commented the farmer. Harold's wrath kindled.

'She is a Londoner. One wouldn't expect her to know the price of plants. And Sam Curdle knew that well enough!'

Percy Hodge looked at his companion curiously.

'No offence, old man. I'm not trying to excuse Sam. He's a twister right enough, and he'll get his marching orders in the morning.'

'I can let you have a couple of dozen plants,' said Harold, more coolly, 'if you're short. It seems a pity to worry Mrs Prior about this. She was upset when I told her my suspicions.'

'Well, that's very handsome of you, but I've got all I need really. Tell the lady to leave them where they are, and not to worry her head about the matter. I'll deal with our Sam, you mark my words.'

They walked across to the Land Rover which the farmer had left in the chestnut avenue, and bade each other a cheerful good night.

'That was a rum thing,' mused Percy Hodge to himself, as he drove up the shadowy lane to Nod and Nidden. 'I shouldn't wonder if old Harold Shoosmith isn't a bit sweet on that young woman. Ah well, no fool like an old fool!'

He trod on the accelerator, keen to confront Sam Curdle with the fruits of this chance encounter.

Suddenly, the thought of his farmyard, free of the Curdle tribe for ever, filled him with pleasurable relief.

Harold Shoosmith's flash of anger surprised the man himself quite as much as it surprised the observant farmer.

He returned thoughtfully to his quiet house and sank into an armchair. What exactly was happening to him? He didn't mind admitting that he was attracted to Phil Prior, but then he had been attracted to many girls in the past. He had always enjoyed the company of intelligent women, and if they were pretty, then so much the better. This protective feeling for Phil Prior, he told himself, was the result of her unfortunate circumstances. Anyone with a spark of humanity would want to help a poor girl left defenceless and hard up, especially when she had to cope with the rearing of a young child, single-handed.

Sam Curdle's was such a dirty trick! He grew warm again at the very thought. It was small wonder that he flared up in Hodge's company. Any decent man would.

Or would he? Harold rose from the chair and walked restlessly about the room. Was he really becoming fonder of this girl than he realized? Damn it all, this was absurd! He was a steadfast bachelor and intended to remain so. He was old enough to be Phil's father. Well, nearly –

He walked to the end of the room and studied his reflection in the handsome gilt-framed mirror which lay above the little Sheraton side-table.

He was tall and spare, his eyes bright, and his hair, although silver, still thick. As a young man he had been reckoned good-looking. He supposed now, trying to look at himself dis-passionately, he still had a few good points – but he was old, old, old, he told himself sternly. No young woman would consider him now, and quite right too!

He returned to his chair, dismissing these foolish thoughts, and opened the paper. It was as inspiring and exhilarating as ever. Four young men were appearing on charges of peddling drugs, an old lady had had her hand chopped off whilst attempting to retain her purse, containing two and eightpence, and a motorway to end all motorways was proposed which would wipe out six particularly exquisite villages and several hundred miles of countryside.

Harold threw it to the floor, leant back and closed his eyes. How pleasantly quiet it was! The fire whispered. The clock ticked. Somewhere, across the green, a car changed gear as it moved towards Lulling, and hummed away into nothingness. This was what he had looked forward to throughout those long hard years of business life in Africa. He would be mad to try and change his way of life now.

And yet Charles Henstock had found a great deal of happiness in later life since his marriage to Dimity. Charles, Harold pointed out to himself, had nothing to lose when he married. Ruled by that dreadful old harridan Mrs Butler, that desiccated Scotswoman who half-starved the poor rector, enduring the chilly discomfort of that great barn of a rectory all alone – of course marriage was attractive! Besides, Charles was the sort of man who *should* be married: he was not. That was the crux of the matter.

He took up the poker and turned over a log carefully. Watching the flames shoot up the chimney, he told himself firmly that marriage was out of the question. Once that poor girl's divorce was through he hoped that some decent kind *young* man would appear to make her happy, and take some of her present burdens from her.

Meanwhile, he would do what he could to help her, and would frankly face the fact that her presence gave him enormous pleasure. But for her sake, he must guard his feelings, he reminded himself. Thrush Green was adept at putting two and two together and making five, and she had enough to contend with already, without being annoyed by foolish gossip.

'Avuncular kindness!' said Harold aloud, and was immediately revolted by the phrase. He hit the flaring log such a hefty thwack that it broke in two, dropped the poker, and went to pour himself a much-needed drink.

10. *Harold is in Trouble*

REGRETTABLY, but understandably, Thrush Green folk tended to avoid Dotty Harmer when they saw her approaching. Few had the time to stand and listen to her diatribes against juvenile delinquency, the present-day teaching of history, air pollution, the exploitation of animals or whatever subject happened to be to the fore of Dotty's raggle-taggle mind.

Now that Dotty had kittens to find homes for, the pursuit of her neighbours was doubly frightening to them. Even she, unobservant as she was, began to notice how people hurried away at her approach.

'Can't understand it,' she told Ella, one gloomy November afternoon. She was carrying the daily bottle of goat's milk to her friend's house.

'Anyone'd think I'd got the plague,' she complained, putting the damp bottle down upon the freshly-polished dining table. 'What's wrong?'

'Kittens,' said Ella briefly. 'How many left?'

'Three,' replied Dotty. She looked accusingly at Ella. 'I was relying on you to help me find homes. What about Dimity? Although I still think that house is too draughty for cats. They need warmth, you know.'

'Better a chilly rectory than a watery death,' said Ella downrightly. 'Sam Curdle would drown them for you, I expect, if you're really stuck.'

Dotty blew out her papery old cheeks with indignation.

'The very idea, Ella Bembridge! If that's your idea of a joke, I consider it in particularly poor taste!'

'Don't be stuffy,' said Ella, 'and sit down, for Pete's sake, mopping and mowing about, with the door open too. It's downright unnerving.'

She slammed the door shut, and watched Dotty perch herself primly on the edge of a chair, the epitome of one who has taken umbrage and is rather enjoying it.

'To tell you the truth, Dotty, I clean forgot to ask Dim about the cat. Anyway, I've an idea that Charles is allergic to them. He certainly never had one while Mrs Butler was with him.'

'*That* woman,' said Dotty, 'wouldn't have had *anything* in the house if she'd had her way! I certainly shouldn't have let any cat of mine go there with *her* in charge of the domestic arrangements. It would have been fed on cold potato and bread crusts, I have no doubt – with watered milk to drink. A quite dreadful person! She once had the temerity to offer me a helping of bread pudding to take home. She got short shrift from me, I can tell you. "Throw it to the birds, Mrs Butler," I told her. "If they're strong enough to lift it from the ground they are welcome to it." She wasn't very pleased, I remember.'

'She's got a post as cook in a boys' school, I hear,' said Ella conversationally.

'Dotheboys Hall, no doubt,' commented Dotty sharply, unwinding a long woolly scarf from her skinny neck.

'Have a cup of tea,' suggested Ella, glad to see that her old friend's wrath was subsiding.

'Thank you, dear. That would be most acceptable,' said Dotty graciously, unskewering her hat and placing two formidable hat-pins upright in the arm of her chair, where they quivered like antennae.

'Tell you what,' said Ella, using one of her favourite phrases, as she returned from the kitchen with the tray. 'Let's go over to Dimity's when we've had this. And what about that Mrs Prior? She might like a kitten. Have you tried her?'

'Now, that's quite a good idea,' replied Dotty, picking over the biscuits thoughtfully. 'No, dear, not Petit Beurre. I find them rather too rich. Ah, an Osborne! Just what I love, and a happy reminder of dear Victoria!'

She nibbled happily, and Ella thought, not for the first time, that there was something infinitely endearing about Dotty's innocent pleasure in simple things. Anyone who could wax enthusiastic about an Osborne biscuit commanded Ella's respect.

When their light repast was over, the two ladies crossed to

the rectory to find the rector and his wife sitting by their fire, winding wool.

'A new waistcoat for Charles,' said Dimity. 'Do sit down.'

Ella, as usual, came to the point at once.

'Forgot to ask you before, but do you want one of Dotty's kittens?'

To her surprise, Dimity looked distressed and gazed at her husband.

'Well – ,' she began timidly.

'I should simply love one,' said the rector. 'But Dimity—'

'But *I* should love one too,' cried his wife, 'but I always thought you disliked cats – that you had hay fever or something when they were in the house. Wasn't that why you never had one here?'

'Mrs Butler was the reason why I didn't have one,' said Charles robustly. 'Somehow, I've always thought *you* didn't really want one, and so I've never mentioned it.'

'For two grown people, you really are pretty stupid,' scolded Ella. 'All this sparing each other's feelings can only lead to misunderstandings, as you see. You should speak your mind.'

'Then I take it,' said Dotty, pulling out a crumpled notebook in a business-like manner, 'that you want one.'

'Yes, please,' said Charles and Dimity in unison, smiling at each other.

'Male or female?'

'Do you know which is which?'

'Well, frankly, no!' confessed Dotty, suddenly becoming less business-like.

'In that case,' said the rector, 'we'll be happy to leave it to the vet, when the time comes.'

'Now, I'm very glad to hear you say that,' said Dotty, lowering the indelible pencil which she had been sucking. Her blue-stained lips and tongue gave added piquancy to her appearance.

'I was so afraid you might have religious scruples, Charles, about interfering with nature. I'm glad to see you are more enlightened.'

'Better to give one doctored cat a home, than twenty kittens an untimely end,' said the rector philosophically.

'Quite, quite!' agreed Dotty, turning the pages of her notebook briskly. 'Well, which is it to be? Ginger with white paws, black with white paws, or plain tabby with exceptionally fine eyes?'

The rector and his wife exchanged amused glances.

'We'll come and see them tomorrow,' promised Dimity, 'and pick ours, shall we?'

'Very well,' said Dotty, stuffing the book untidily into her coat pocket. 'Come to tea – you too, Ella dear – and it will save me bringing up the goat's milk.'

'I think,' said the rector, making his way to the sideboard, 'that this transaction should be celebrated with a drink.'

And so it was.

Harold Shoosmith finished his labour of love on the flower border at Tullivers, just before the first sharp frosts of winter arrived. There was still plenty of work in the garden to warrant many more visits, but he was beginning to wonder if it would be wiser to pay calls less frequently.

His heart-searchings had left him somewhat ruefully amused. He was certainly becoming extremely fond of Phil, and Thrush Green must not know it. Nor, of course, must the girl, particularly with divorce proceedings in the offing. Life, thought Harold, cleaning the prongs of his gardening fork, was quite complicated enough without tangling it even more.

He was admiring the tidy border as Willie Bond, the postman, came with the afternoon letters. Phil came to the door to collect them, then crossed the grass to admire his handiwork.

'It really is splendid,' she said truthfully. 'So neat – and so lovely to find that it's got such a lot of good stuff in it already.'

She waved one of her letters.

'Do you mind if I open this now? It's from your friend Frank. Perhaps he's taken something after all.'

She ripped open the envelope and read the contents. Harold watched her growing pink with excitement. She thrust the letter towards him.

'There! Isn't that marvellous? Fifty guineas! I can't believe it.'

'Congratulations,' said Harold warmly. 'Which story is this?'

'Oh, the one about the two friends and the curate,' said Phil. 'I've a copy on the table if you're interested. When do you think they'll publish it? Shall I get paid on acceptance, do you think?'

'I should tell Frank that's what you want,' replied Harold, shouldering his tools. 'And, yes, please, I'd love to read the story.'

'You must have brought it luck,' said the girl when she handed it over. 'You posted it for me. Remember?'

'So I did,' said Harold. 'I've a strong share in this success.'

He made his way back across the green, warmed with the thought of the girl's pleasure. When he had changed, and was sitting by his fire, he settled back to read the story.

He turned the typed pages with growing dismay. It was not the telling of the tale which worried him. Phil's style was as crisp and lucid as always, and the suspense was well-sustained. But the characters, in this present story, were far too realistically portrayed for Harold's peace of mind.

Here, for all the world to see, were Ella and Dimity, in the guise of Jean and Phoebe, and Charles Henstock – though far less attractive – under the name of Tobias Fuller, a hearty curate.

Even their appearance fitted. Jean was thickset, Phoebe skinny. Their determined pursuit of the innocent curate was told with a nice sense of the ridiculous which Harold would have appreciated in different circumstances.

He read it through to the end, let the typescript drop to his knees, and gazed thoughtfully at the fire. This simply must not be printed. He must go and see Phil immediately, before she wrote to accept the offer of payment.

But what a kettle of fish! What could have possessed the girl to lift two characters from life so inartistically! He looked through the story again, and sighing, went to the telephone.

Phil answered immediately.

'Do you think I might come over for a few minutes? It's about the story.'

'Of course. Something wrong with it?'

'Frankly, yes.'

There was a short silence. Then Phil spoke briskly.

'Well, bring it over with you, and we'll go through it. I expect it can be altered easily enough.'

She showed him into the sitting-room where a log fire crackled welcomingly.

'No Jeremy?' asked Harold.

'Early bed tonight. He's running a slight temperature. But he's quite happy reading a Paddington Bear book.'

'I'll go and see him, if I may, before I go.'

'He'd love that. But do tell me – you can guess how anxious I am – what's the matter with the story?'

Harold found her bright gaze very difficult to face.

'If you want to continue to live at Thrush Green,' said Harold, 'I'm afraid you'll have to scrap it.'

'Scrap it?' cried Phil, in horror. 'But why?'

'Jean and Phoebe are Ella and Dimity to a T. The curate, though not so near the knuckle, might be Charles Henstock.'

The girl looked aghast.

'I never thought of that,' she whispered. 'Here's a how-d'you-do.'

She looked swiftly at Harold and put a hand upon his arm.

'You surely don't think I did this knowingly? I wrote that story three years ago – long before I knew anyone here. Don't you remember? You said it would be a good idea to send a story I had by me while I altered the new one. This is it.'

'I remember very well.'

'What on earth shall I do?'

'Tell Frank to send it back.'

Phil's face took on a mutinous look.

'I don't really see why I should. I've got a clear conscience. This is pure coincidence. Frank's accepted it, and I'm dam' glad to have earned fifty guineas. Besides Frank won't be particularly anxious to take other things if I mess him about with this effort.'

Harold said nothing.

'Besides,' continued Phil, getting up and walking restlessly about the room, 'how many people in Thrush Green are likely to see this particular magazine? And what the hell does it matter if someone thinks I've written about Ella and Dimity? I wrote that story in good faith, and the money's honestly earned. And, believe me, it's needed. I've just had a further bill from the wretched builders for eighty-five pounds. This isn't the time to start being squeamish about possible hurt feelings.'

Harold let her argue herself to a standstill. Soon enough, he realized, she would be able to cope with this bitter disappointment, and he felt sure that she would decide, eventually, to withdraw the offending story.

'I really think you are fussing about nothing,' she went on standing in front of his chair. 'Why must you be so maddeningly interfering? The implications would never have dawned on me – and I don't suppose, for one minute, that they ever will on any readers in Thrush Green – if there are any. Why did you have to meddle in this?'

'Because I don't want to see you leaving Tullivers,' said Harold drily.

Phil snorted.

'It would take more than a few wagging tongues to oust me from Thrush Green, I can assure you.'

She sat down abruptly in the armchair on the opposite side of the hearth. Harold could see that her fury was fast abating. Far more upsetting, to his tender heart, was the look of hurt bewilderment which began to creep across her countenance.

'What on earth shall I do?' she asked quietly. 'I could, I suppose, have it published under a pen name.'

She sounded near to tears, and Harold began to feel alarmed about his own ability to cope with an emotional situation. If only she weren't so confoundedly pretty, it would be easier, he told himself.

'I feel partly to blame,' he said. 'Shall I have a word with Frank and say that I've noticed this likeness?'

'No, thanks,' replied Phil shortly. 'I can handle it.'

Harold refused to feel rebuffed.

'Very well. But you do see that it would be far wiser to scrap the story?'

'No, I can't say I do. And I'm not making up my mind one way or the other until the morning.'

'I'm glad to hear it.'

'I think you meant well – '

'Thanks,' interjected Harold grimly.

'But I don't relish your interference, I must say. I've nothing to blame myself for, and I need the money. Naturally, I don't want to upset good neighbours, but I'm not keen on upsetting Frank either.'

She stood up, and Harold rose to make his departure.

'No hard feelings?' he said with a smile.

'Of course not.' Her tone was warm.

'And can I see the boy?'

'Yes, indeed. Let's go up.'

But when they reached the bedroom the child was asleep with the open book lodged upon his chest.

Phil removed it quietly, put out the bedside light and they went downstairs.

'By the way,' said the girl. 'We're going to have a cat.'

'One of Dotty's?'

'That's right. Jeremy's thrilled.'

'And what about you?'

'Modified rapture. I love them, but I'm terrified of the traffic, and we're so horribly near the road.'

'Keep your fingers crossed,' said Harold, on the doorstep. He hesitated for a moment.

'Will you be kind enough to let me know how you decide to act?' he said diffidently. 'Perhaps I shouldn't interfere any more.'

'I shall let you know as soon as I've made up my mind,' said Phil stiffly. She watched him make his way to the gate, raised her hand in farewell, and closed the door, with what seemed to Harold, unnecessary firmness.

'Damn!' said Harold, plodding homeward. A much-quoted dictum of his old nurse's floated into his perplexed mind.

'What can't be cured must be endured!'

Cold comfort indeed, thought Harold, turning the key in his front door.

Harold Shoosmith was not the only person in the neighbourhood to suffer a disturbed night.

Sam Curdle was receiving the lashing of Bella's tongue, as they packed their few poor belongings in the stuffy caravan. They were off at first light, making for a village north of Southampton.

Bella had learned the bitter truth that they were to depart from the farmer's wife.

'I'm sorry to lose you, Bella,' Mrs Hodge said truthfully. 'You've been a good worker and we've got on well. But my husband won't be done, as you know, and Sam's a fool to try it on.'

Bella had pleaded for leniency, promising to keep an eye on her erring husband, although she knew, in her heart, that he was too slippery a customer even for her control. The poor woman was at her wits' end. There were three children to bring up and she knew that Sam's chances of getting any kind of job in the Thrush Green area were slight indeed.

Mrs Hodge stood firm. It was as much as her life was worth, she said, to oppose Percy. Sam had known from the start that he was allowed in the yard on sufferance. He had flouted the master's demands, and there was an end to it.

A furious scene between Sam and Bella followed. The next day, Bella, slightly less heated, betook herself to the telephone booth at the corner of Thrush Green, a fine assortment of coins in hand.

Unknown to Sam, whom she had left sulking in bed, she put her pride in her pocket and decided to talk to her father who kept a country pub in a village in Hampshire. She had been his barmaid before marriage, and hoped that he and her stepmother would take pity on their plight now.

She disliked the idea of going there intensely, but there seemed to be no alternative. Her father had married some years after the death of Bella's mother, and her step-mother was a hard-working, but tight-fisted woman who had never taken particularly to her blowsy step-daughter. It wouldn't be a very comfortable situation for the Curdle family, Bella knew, remembering her step-mother's sharp tongue, but beggars couldn't be choosers, she told herself, as she dropped the coins in the box.

Her father was a tender-hearted man and responded kindly to her tearful call for help. Yes, they could all come, and the caravan could stand in the backyard. As it happened, his present barmaid was leaving to have a baby, though she would be back in a couple of months, Bella must understand.

And Maud herself, Bella's step-mother, was laid up with a sprained ankle, so Bella would be doubly welcome.

Sam, said her father, with rather less warmth, could find himself a job nearby and could earn a few bob helping him in the evenings with the crates.

'But you can tell him straight, Bella, he's to behave himself. You know what I mean. You and the kids are welcome for a bit, just to tide you over like, but Sam had better get down to a steady job and make a proper home for you all. Tell him I said so.'

Bella promised, with some relish, thanked her father sincerely and went back to the caravan to face Sam with the ultimatum.

'Well, we ain't going!' said Sam roundly, when faced with the news.

A dangerous glint appeared in Bella's eye, and Sam began to quail inwardly.

'You speak for yourself, Sam Curdle. Go where you like – it don't trouble me, and that's flat. But me and the kids set off tomorrow for home. I can drive well enough to get us down there, and I reckons I own this caravan more than you do. It's my wages as keeps us going, and we'll all be a dam' sight better off without you.'

'Now, Bella – ' began Sam.

Scarlet in the face, Bella rounded upon him.

'Take it or leave it! We're off first thing tomorrow, come rain or shine. Come if you like, or clear off – one or the other!'

And so, next morning, the battered caravan clattered out of Percy Hodge's yard for ever. As it rattled by Harold

Shoosmith's house, Willie Bond the postman watched it. At the wheel was a grim-faced Sam. Beside him, arms folded, sat an equally grim-faced Bella. The news that the Curdles were off had already flown around the neighbourhood, but Willie was the only witness to their departure.

'Good riddance to bad rubbish!' said Willie aloud, as the caravan slid out of sight down the steep hill to Lulling.

He echoed the general feelings of Thrush Green.

HAROLD Shoosmith's bathroom was at the back of the house overlooking the little valley that lay to the west of Thrush Green. In the distance were Lulling Woods, a deep blue smudge against the winter sky.

As he shaved the next morning he gazed beyond the shaving mirror on the window sill observing the bare trees and brindled hedges of winter. The elm trees, near Dotty Harmer's distant cottage, spread their fans of black lace, and a wisp of blue smoke, curling up towards them, showed that Dotty was already astir.

After his restless night, Harold felt out of sorts. He had gone over the irritating affair of Phil's story, time and time again, in the maddening way one does at night. He had almost decided, at one stage, to ignore Phil's request to cease meddling and to ring Frank and explain matters, swearing his old friend to secrecy.

But with morning light, things could be seen more coolly, and Harold made up his mind to let this business work itself out, without worrying himself unduly. He had made his point. It was Phil's decision, and she had plenty of sense.

He determined to put it at the back of his mind, and went downstairs to brew his coffee and make toast. Nevertheless, he intended to keep within earshot of the telephone. Luckily, Betty Bell came that day to go through the house, like a mighty rushing wind, and she would answer the telephone if Harold were called away unexpectedly.

For the first part of the morning he worked at his desk, the telephone within arm's reach. It rang once and he snatched it up, only to be told that the exchange was testing his line.

Betty Bell burst in, without knocking, at eleven o'clock, bearing half a cup and half a saucerful of far too milky coffee, and two soggy gingernuts.

'Heard the news?' she asked.

'What about?'

'Them Curdles.'

'I heard Percy Hodge had asked them to leave,' said Harold guardedly.

'Fair old rumpus they had, Bella and Sam,' said Betty sitting down on *The Times* which Harold had left in the armchair. 'Willie Bond said they looked as black as thunder going off in that old van. Got a tin bath and the pushchair lashed on top. He said it sounded like Alexander's rag-time band.'

Betty burst into merry laughter, rocking back and forth to the detriment of *The Times*.

'Proper cough-drop old Willie is! You ever heard him sing "I Gotter Motter"?'

'No,' said Harold, pouring the coffee from the saucer into the cup. The biscuits he had wrapped in blotting paper and deposited in the waste-paper basket.

'You ought! You really ought! Brings the house down. Never fails. Always gets an encore, does Willie.'

She got up bouncily.

'Well, this won't buy the baby a new frock, will it? I'm doing you liver and bacon for your dinner. All right?'

Harold nodded. Betty Bell, in full spate, after a poor night, was more than usually exhausting.

She whirled out, crashing the door behind her. Harold sipped his tepid coffee and looked across the green to Tullivers. What was going on there?

A pale wintry sun lit the scene. He decided that he would do some gardening. No point in moping about. Fresh air and exercise would do him good.

'Give an ear to the phone, Betty,' he said casually, as he dragged on his wellingtons. 'I'm expecting a call.'

But it did not come. The morning passed. The liver and bacon were cooked and eaten. Betty Bell departed, leaving her master hoeing the beds beneath the study window where the telephone bell could be heard should it happen to ring.

But it remained silent for the rest of the day, and when evening came Harold shrugged aside the whole stupid incident and bent his energies to solving a much-crumpled crossword puzzle in *The Times*.

The departure of Sam and Bella Curdle had repercussions in the community. John Donne's dictum about no man being an island is truer in a village, perhaps, than in any larger community.

In the first place, Winnie Bailey was expecting him to come to the house to sweep the kitchen chimney. An odd quirk in this structure, necessitated by a by-gone architect's devious design, meant that it needed a sweep's ministrations twice a year. Dr Bailey owned some stout brushes, which were frequently loaned to neighbours, for this purpose, and Sam was always ready to do the job for five shillings.

Albert Piggott was the second person to miss Sam. They had been instructed by the rector to take out some rusty and damaged iron palings from the churchyard fence.

'Children or animals could be injured so easily,' said the rector anxiously. His sexton had snorted, but made no spoken comment. Children and animals, his expression implied, got what they deserved if they meddled.

'It's too bad,' said Mrs Bailey, when she heard that Sam had gone. 'That wretched boiler will start smoking as soon as the wind changes, mark my words. I shall have to get someone up from Lulling, I suppose.'

'No need,' said Richard, sprinkling wheat germ on his plate of Otto-recommended breakfast cereal. 'I'll do it this evening.'

Winnie surveyed her neat nephew with new respect.

'Do you know what to do?'

'Of course. I rather like sweeping chimneys. And cleaning drains. So worthwhile. Instant rewards, you know.'

He poured himself some coffee.

'Think no more of it. I'll be ready for the job after dinner tonight, if that suits you.'

'Wonderful!' cried Winnie. 'I'm most grateful, Richard dear. I'll let the boiler out this afternoon.'

True to his word, Richard tackled the job that evening. He was clad in ex-R.A.F. overalls, once white, but now mottled with the stains of many a year and many a job, from creosoting fences to cleaning out wells.

'They go everywhere with me,' said Richard, stroking his filthy overalls fondly. 'Such a useful rig-out.'

This practical side of Richard's nature was new to his aunt, and she found her respect for the young man growing considerably as she watched him tackling the flue. He was quick and clean. He had had the forethought to spread newspapers at strategic points, and he wasted no time in idle conversation as Sam Curdle did.

While the flue brush was rattling away inside the chimney, Phil Prior called.

'My goodness,' she said, with admiration. 'You're making a splendid job of that.'

'A minor accomplishment,' replied Richard, with a rare smile. 'It's more useful than painting water-colours these days.'

'It certainly is,' agreed the girl. She turned to Mrs Bailey.

'I hate to bother you, but would you come and have a look at Jeremy? He's looking so flushed. He went to sleep as usual, but he's woken up again so crotchety. I don't like to bother Doctor Lovell, but if you think – '

'Let me slip on my coat,' said Mrs Bailey, making for the stairs.

'Ah!' said Richard, with enormous satisfaction. A sizeable piece of hardened soot rattled down the chimney and splintered on the waiting newspaper.

'I think Aunt Winnie wants a different sort of fuel for this contraption.'

He picked up the soot in a blackened hand and studied it with close attention. Phil watched, amused. At last, this young man had come to life! Until then, she had found him cold and a trifle supercilious.

'Do you often sweep chimneys?' she asked lightly.

'If I'm asked I do,' replied Richard. 'I like mucky jobs. It makes a change from my finicky figure work.'

He looked at her swiftly.

'Do you want anything done?'

'Not chimneys, alas. They were done when we moved in, but –' She hesitated.

'No, nothing really,' she finished lamely.

'It's a waste-pipe,' said Richard shrewdly.

Phil laughed.

'You're clairvoyant! As a matter of fact, it is.'

'Well, I love a good stuffed-up waste-pipe,' said Richard, with relish. 'I'll be over tomorrow evening, if that suits you.'

'There's no hurry – it's the spare room waste-pipe, but I'd be eternally grateful, if you really mean to do it.'

'Mean to do it? Of course, I mean to do it,' said Richard indignantly. 'If not tomorrow, then one evening soon. I'll ring first to see if it's convenient.'

'You are kind,' said Phil gratefully.

Mrs Bailey reappeared and the two women hurried next door. After inspecting Jeremy, Winnie suggested a little milk of magnesia.

'And if he still seems feverish in the morning, send for Doctor Lovell. He'll pop in before morning surgery, no doubt.'

'You've relieved my mind,' said the girl. 'I seem to worry unnecessarily.'

'How are things going?' Winnie ventured.

'Worse,' said Phil. 'By that I mean that the wheels are grinding along. What I *cannot bear* is the thought of Christmas for Jeremy without his father. I must screw myself to telling him before long. I can't tell you how I dread it.'

'Do you hear from him?'

'Sometimes he writes a short note when he sends my cheque. He's in France, at the moment. With her, I imagine.'

The girl sounded dog-tired and hopeless. Winnie felt powerless to help.

'And the writing?' she asked, hoping to find a more cheerful topic.

Phil laughed mirthlessly.

'All in a muddle. I've had an acceptance, but I'm not sure if I want it to be published now. There are plenty of stories, by me, waiting to be read by editors. Something may turn up.'

'I'm sure it will,' said Winnie robustly. 'Now have an early night, and by morning both you and Jeremy will be fighting fit again.'

She kissed her gently, and returned home, shaking her head. 'Poor young thing!' she murmured, opening the kitchen door.

Richard was taking up the newspapers. The stove was back to rights and freshly-washed.

'That's a nice young woman,' observed Richard thoughtfully. 'Is her divorce through yet?'

My goodness, thought Winnie, in some alarm, Richard's touch may be sure enough with chimneys and waste-pipes, but it was surely rather too heavy and direct in his dealings with women!

Albert Piggott did not find help as easily as Winnie Bailey.

He surveyed the cold November day through his cottage window. It was going to be proper bleak tugging up them old railings. Been stuck there, in Cotswold clay, for a hundred years. They'd take some shifting – and no Sam to give him a hand.

He said as much to Nelly, who was whirling about behind him with a tin of polish and a duster. He got short shrift from her.

'A good day's work won't hurt you, Albert. Make a nice change,' she puffed, rubbing energetically at the top of the table. 'Do that liver of yours a power of good.'

Fat lot of sympathy she ever gives me, thought Albert morosely, lifting his greasy cap from the peg behind the door. He dressed slowly, watching his buxom wife attacking the furniture with zest.

All right for some, Albert grumbled to himself, crossing to the windy churchyard. She'd never had a day's illness in her life – strong as a horse, she was – and still game to make eyes at that oilman.

The pain which gnawed intermittently at Albert's inside seemed worse today. Doctor Lovell's pills helped a little, but Nelly's food was too rich, no doubt about it, and he was that starved with hunger when it came to meal times, he ate whatever she provided, dreading too the lash of her tongue if he refused to eat.

He set about the broken railings and found the job as difficult as he had feared. As he tugged he contemplated his marriage. What a fool he'd been! A clean house and good cooking was no exchange for peace and quiet, and that was what he missed. The only times he had the house to himself were Tuesdays and Fridays when Nelly took herself to Bingo at Lulling.

Or did she? A sudden suspicion made Albert straighten his back and look across Thrush Green. Come to think of it, Bingo was on Saturday night. It dawned, with horrible clarity, on Albert's dull mind, that Nelly must be meeting the oilman on Tuesdays and Fridays.

That was it! Tuesday was the oilman's half-day, he remembered, and Friday was his pay-day. It all fitted together.

He bent to his task again, half relishing the scene when he confronted Nelly with his discovery. The pain in his stomach seemed worse, and there was a tight feeling across his chest which he had not suffered before, but he continued tugging with the vigour born of righteous indignation.

He saw Nelly whisk out of the cottage, a basket on her arm, bound for the butcher's down the hill. He gave her no greeting, but watched sourly as her ample back vanished in the distance.

'You wait, my gal,' said Albert grimly. 'You just wait!'

Young Jeremy Prior was no better the next morning and Doctor Lovell called at Tullivers when morning surgery, next door, was over.

'There's measles about,' he told Phil when they were downstairs again, 'but it doesn't look like it at the moment. No rash yet, of course. But keep him in bed, and I'll look in tomorrow.'

He eyed the girl sympathetically. She looked wretchedly tired.

'Did you sleep last night?'

'Not much.'

'Would you like a few tablets?'

'Not really, many thanks. I've a horror of pills, and I know

I'll have a good night tonight. It works out that way, I find.'

'Good,' said the young doctor briskly. 'But if I can help, do just say. And don't worry about that young man upstairs. I think we'll find his temperature's down tomorrow.'

Throughout the day the child was unusually demanding and fractious. He wanted his mother with him most of the time, and she was content to shelve her writing and sit beside him reading stories or helping with a gigantic ancient jig-saw puzzle of the Wembley Exhibition, bequeathed to him by Winnie Bailey.

The affair of the story niggled at the back of her mind, but she had little time to give it attention that day. Harold Shoo-smith's attitude she still found high-handed, and was annoyed that she cared so much. The fact that he might expect to hear about her decision that day, never entered her head. She had told him that she would let him know what she would do, and this she intended to do in time.

Meanwhile, she kept Jeremy company and watched the activities of her neighbours through the bedroom window. She saw Albert Piggott attacking the church railings, and his fat wife waddling down the road. She saw Charles Henstock walking across the green, bent against the wind, to speak to Albert. Her friend, Joan Young, emerged from the fine house nearby, and battled her way towards Lulling, and across the green she watched the children pour into the playground at mid-morning, shouting and leaping, whilst little Miss Fogerty stood sipping her tea among the tumult.

It reminded Phil that she must let Miss Watson know why Jeremy was away. She would telephone during the dinner hour. She did not want to be out of earshot if Jeremy called.

But in the afternoon, when he fell into a peaceful sleep, she ventured into the garden to get a breath of the cold blustery air. A rose or two still starred the bushes and she picked them to enjoy indoors. The winter jasmine was in bud and already one or two bulbs were poking their green shoots through the earth.

Elsewhere winter held sway. The chestnut trees were bare now, in the avenue, and the dead leaves of the Baileys' beech hedge rustled dryly in the wind. The skeletons of dead plants rattled together like castanets, and the matted ivy on the old wall flapped up and down like a loose curtain.

The Cotswold stone was as grey as the November sky above it. In the distance, the girl could see the dun-coloured meadows of winter and the faraway smudge of Lulling Woods. The grey coldness seemed to echo her own life just now. Would she ever know light and warmth, colour and excitement again? Would this desolation last for ever?

She was tired of the struggling, tired of keeping up a bright front for Jeremy, for the neighbours and for herself. If only something, however insignificant, would happen to give her hope.

12. *Albert is Struck Down*

THE wind increased to a gale during the night, screaming down the hill to Lulling, rattling windows and even shifting some of the heavy stone roof tiles of the town. The few remaining leaves were wrenched from the trees, and an old oak crashed across the road near Percy Hodge's farm, bringing down some telephone wires, and causing more than usual confusion in the Lulling exchange.

It was no better in the morning. Willie Marchant could make no headway on his bicycle in the face of this fierce northerly blast. Even his tacking methods were no use against it, and he was forced to wheel his bicycle up the steep hill, his eyes half shut against the cigarette ash which blew dangerously against his face from the inevitable stub in his mouth.

It was useless to try to prop a bicycle against the kerb in this wind, and when he reached Tullivers he prudently lodged it against the wall while he battled his way up the path.

There was no one about, and he thrust the letters through the flap beneath the admiral's dolphin and continued on his erratic course.

Everywhere he met tales of damage. A flying tile had broken the glass in Joan Young's greenhouse. The school dustbin had been found in the hedge at the end of the playground. Albert Piggott's cat was missing, 'blown to kingdom-come', its owner surmised gloomily.

Little Miss Fogerty did not tell Willie about her own troubles, but they had been severe. Two pairs of sensible long-legged knickers, of a style which she had been brought up to know as 'directoire', had blown from the discreet little clothes line hidden by laurel trees, over the hedge into her neighbour's garden.

Much agitated, she had watched until the man of the house had gone to work, and then had knocked timidly at Mrs Bates' door to explain about her embarrassing loss. Mrs Bates, a kind-hearted woman, forbore to show any coarse amusement, as some less refined Thrush Green folk might have done, rescued the garments from the roof of her hen-house and returned them gravely, wrapping them first in a piece of brown paper. Miss Fogerty was much touched by the delicacy of this gesture, but the horror of the incident haunted her for the rest of the day.

Harold Shoosmith heard about the havoc in the Lulling Woods area when Betty Bell burst into his house at half-past nine.

'I found Miss Harmer's letters all twizzled up in her string bag in the road. Soaking wet, of course, but it never bothered her. "They'll dry, dear," was all she said when I took 'em into her. Willie won't be best pleased, I'll lay. And the roof blew off the hen-house at "The Drovers' Arms" and landed in the pond! My, what a night! Any damage here?'

Harold had to admit that he had found none. Betty looked disappointed. She thrived on daily drama.

It was later that morning that the telephone rang, and Harold's spirits soared when he heard the excitement in Phil's voice.

'Wonderful news! Frank's taken the latest story, and for more money.'

'I'm so glad. Well done!'

'Isn't it splendid? And he wants me to meet him "with a view to further work", so his letter says. I'm going to ring him in a few minutes.'

'You'll find him very easy to talk to,' said Harold. 'What's more, he can explain the sort of thing he wants done, which saves a lot of time and temper.'

He paused, wondering if the girl would tell him about the awkward story. As if she knew his thoughts, she spoke of it next.

'I've decided to scrap that other thing. You were quite right.'

'That's extremely generous of you.'

'Not at all. It could have upset people here – though I still think the chances were slight, particularly if I'd used a pen-name. Anyway, this second acceptance takes care of most of the builder's bill, and I don't feel so hard-pressed.'

'I can't tell you how pleased I am,' said Harold warmly. 'You deserve to succeed. You've worked so hard lately.'

'I hope you weren't expecting a call yesterday,' said Phil suddenly. 'Jeremy was off-colour and I didn't really bother much about the other problem. He's much better this morning, thank goodness, but won't go to school until next week.'

'Well, give the young man my regards,' said Harold. 'Now, I'm not going to hold you up – you must be anxious to get in touch with Frank. Remember me to him, if it enters your head. I hope he'll come down here one day. Meanwhile, the best of luck with all your ploys.'

He put down the receiver, feeling unusually elated. It was a relief to know that the story would never appear, and even more gratifying to know that the girl was having some success. Frank would treat her right, thought Harold robustly!

He went into the windy garden, whistling like a boy, and Betty Bell, well-versed in affairs of the heart, winked at her reflection in the hall mirror as she polished it.

Richard was as good as his word and appeared some evenings later dressed in his working overalls and carrying his drain-clearing equipment. His expression was animated, and when Phil opened the door to him she was struck by his good looks, which she had not noticed before.

'Got plenty of newspaper?' asked Richard, mounting the stairs. 'I like lashings of *really thick* paper to spread about.'

'About a dozen *Telegraphs* and great fat wads of *Sunday Times*,' said Phil. 'And all those lovely Business Supplements no one reads. Absolutely unopened, they are.'

'Good, good! Pity you don't take the *Sunday Express* though. Wonderful powers of absorption for this sort of job.'

He spread the papers busily, patting them down happily, and humming to himself. It was quite obvious to Phil that he would be better alone with his passion.

'I'll get out of your way,' she said diplomatically, 'but shout if you want anything.'

She heard nothing for the next twenty minutes but the sound of running water and Richard's footsteps up and down the stairs as he hurried outside to make sure that the water was flowing without interruption. When he finally appeared in the sitting-room, he looked triumphant.

'As I thought, simply the U-bend. No difficulty at all. Someone has been using a disintegrating face-flannel, I suspect.'

'Not guilty,' smiled Phil. 'Perhaps the admiral's sister? I believe she used that room.'

She indicated a tray of drinks on a low table by the fire.

'What will you have? My goodness, you've earned a drink! I'm so very grateful.'

Richard looked at the pale chair covers, and with rare thoughtfulness began to step out of his filthy overalls. It seemed to Phil, watching him, that this young man wasn't the ogre that Winnie, despite her tact, had portrayed.

'My aunt tells me that you write,' said Richard. He sipped his dry sherry appreciatively. Otto allowed one small sherry a day if it were a dry one, Richard remembered happily.

'Not as successfully as I should like,' admitted Phil, 'but it all helps. I'm hoping for some more work next Wednesday.'

She told him about Frank.

'Wednesday,' repeated Richard. 'I'm going to town myself that day. Let me run you up. What time do you have to meet him?'

Phil told him that she was lunching with Frank and that she had planned to catch the 10.10 train from Lulling, changing at Oxford, as her car was needing attention.

'It will give me time to see Jeremy safely to school and to tidy up here,' she said. 'Joan Young is having him to lunch, and tea, and I shall collect him about 6.'

'I was proposing to leave about 10.30,' said Richard. 'I am spending the night with the Carslakes, so I'm afraid I can't bring you back, but do please give me the pleasure of your company on the journey up.'

'I should love to,' said the girl, and thought how pleasant it was to be talking to a man of her own age again. A jaunt to London would be something to look forward to after the recent drab weeks at Thrush Green, and Richard she found surprisingly interesting.

He stayed for over an hour and was at his most charming. As he returned to the Baileys' house, carrying his impedimenta, he sniffed the frosty air with relish.

He put his head round the sitting room door. His uncle and aunt surveyed him mildly over their spectacles.

'It's a wonderfully bright night,' said Richard. 'Do you mind if I take a brisk walk?'

'Not at all, dear boy,' said Winnie. 'But don't get over-tired.'

'Tired?' echoed Richard in amazement. 'My dear aunt, I could walk ten miles without stopping tonight!'

He vanished, and they heard the front door slam.

The doctor lowered his newspaper and looked across at his wife.

'Would you think,' he asked pensively, 'that our Richard is putting some of Otto's theories into practice?'

International crises always seem to occur at week-ends. Domestic crises appear to follow the same pattern.

Certainly, there was a crisis at Albert Piggott's home on the Sunday. Nelly had dished up a boiled hand of pork, broad beans, onions and plenty of parsley sauce. She had also excelled herself by providing a Christmas pudding for the second course with a generous helping of brandy butter.

'I made six full-size ones,' said Nelly, surveying the pudding fondly, 'but this little 'un was for a try-out before Christmas. What d'you think of it?'

'All right, if your stummick's up to it,' replied Albert dourly, turning his spoon about in the rich fruitiness.

'Lord love old Ireland!' cried Nelly, in exasperation. 'Ain't you a misery? Small thanks I gets for slaving away over the stove day in and day out. Wouldn't do you no harm to have bread and water for a week.'

'You're right there,' agreed Albert sarcastically. 'You knows full well the doctor said I was to go easy on rich food. I believes you does it apurpose to upset me.'

Nelly rose from the table with surprising swiftness for one of her bulk. She whisked round the table behind her husband, and before he knew what was afoot, she had thrust his head sharply into his plate of pudding.

'*You besom!*' spluttered Albert emerging with a face smothered in the brown mess, and with a badly-bumped nose. He picked up the plate and threw it at his wife. It clattered to the floor, puddingside down, but miraculously did not break.

Nelly, who had dodged successfully, now broke into peals of hysterical laughter as she watched her husband grope his way to the sink to wash off his dessert.

'You wait till I get my hands on you,' threatened Albert. 'I'll beat the living daylights out of you, my gal! Pity I never done it before. You and that oil man!'

Nelly's shrieks of laughter stopped suddenly.

'You can leave him out of this, Albert Piggott. He knows how to treat a lady.'

'Humph!' grunted Albert, from the depths of the roller-towel on the door. 'I'll bet he knows! I could have the law on him, if I'd a mind, carrying on with another man's wife.'

Nelly adopted a superior aloofness.

'I'm not stopping here to listen to your filthy insinuations,' she said loftily. 'I shall go and have a lay-down, and you can clear up this mess you've made with your tantrums.'

'That I won't!' shouted Albert to her departing back. 'I'm due at church at 2.15 for christenings, and you can dam' well clear up your own kitchen!'

The door, slamming behind Nelly, shook the house, and a minute later Albert heard the springs of the bed above squeak under his wife's considerable weight.

Growling, he flung himself into the chair by the fire, picked up the *News of the World*, and prepared to have a quarter of an hour's peace before going across to St Andrew's for his duties.

Hostilities were not resumed until the early evening. Nelly remained upstairs, but ominous thumps and door-bangings proclaimed that she was active. When she re-appeared, she was dressed in her best hat and coat, and was carrying a large suitcase which she set upon the table, taking care to miss the dirty dinner plates and cutlery with which it was still littered.

'Well, Albert, I've had enough,' said Nelly flatly. 'I'm off!'

If she expected any pleading, or even surprise, from her husband she was disappointed. Albert's morose expression remained unchanged.

'Good riddance!' said Albert. 'You asked yourself here and you can go for all I care. But don't come here whining to be took back when that fancy-man of yours has got fed up with you.'

Nelly drew in an outraged breath.

'Come back here? Not if you went down on your bended knees, Albert Piggott, and begged of me! No, not if it was with your dying breath! You've seen the last of me, I can tell you. I'm going where I shall be appreciated!'

She hoisted the case from the table and struggled to the door. Albert remained seated by the fire, the newspaper across his knees, his face surly and implacable.

He remained so for several long minutes, listening to his wife's footsteps dying away as she walked out of his life for ever. He had no doubt that Nelly spoke the truth. Their ways had parted.

He looked at the kitchen clock. Time he went to ring the bell for Evensong.

But when he came to stir himself, the pain across his chest seared him like a red-hot knife. He fell to his knees, his head pillowed on the *News of the World* on the hearth-rug, and was unable to move. The last thing he saw, before the blackness engulfed him, was the remains of the Christmas pudding spattered, dark and glutinous, across the kitchen wall.

The rector, robing in the vestry, realized with alarm, that Piggott was absent.

'You'd better ring the bell,' he told the largest choir-boy. 'Mr Piggott seems to have been held up.'

Privately, Charles Henstock feared that his verger might be the worse for drink. It had happened before, but he did not wish to be uncharitable, and he told himself that he must postpone judgement until he had seen the fellow.

Albert did not appear during the service, and as soon as his few parishioners had departed, Charles put out the lights himself, saw that things were in order, and then crossed to Albert's cottage.

The windows were dark, and the rector feared that Albert was indeed in a stupor. Really, drink was a great nuisance!

He knocked and got no reply.

'Anyone at home?' called the rector, opening the door. The sight that met his eyes, in the gloom, frightened him exceedingly.

He found the light switch and surveyed the chaos. Albert's huddled body lay before the dying fire, but his heavy breathing showed that he was still alive.

'Thank God!' said the rector from his heart, kneeling beside the man. He turned him over, into a more comfortable position and put the cushion from the armchair beneath his head.

'Piggott!' he cried sharply. 'Can you hear me, Piggott?'

A growling sound came from Albert's pale lips, and his eyelids fluttered spasmodically.

'Stay there,' cautioned the rector, thinking, as he said it, how idiotic it was. There was small chance of Albert moving far.

'I'm going for help,' he said, making for the door. The man must have a doctor. Should he telephone from home, or run along to Harold Shoosmith's? There was nothing in it as to distance, and he did not wish to alarm Dimity. Harold it should be.

He ran through the darkness, past 'The Two Pheasants' and was soon banging Harold's knocker.

'My dear chap,' said Harold to his breathless friend. 'What is it? Come in, do.'

'It's Piggott. A seizure or something,' puffed Charles. 'Can I use your telephone?'

'I'll ring Lovell,' said Harold, taking command, 'while you go back. I'll follow as soon as I've got through. And don't worry,' he shouted to his retreating friend, 'it's probably only the drink!'

'Not this time, I fear,' called back the rector, hurrying away.

Twenty minutes later Doctor Lovell agreed with the rector as he surveyed his patient.

The three men had carried Albert up the narrow stairs to his bed. He was conscious now, but very weak and pale.

'We've got an ambulance on the way for you, Albert,' said Doctor Lovell. 'I want to have a proper look at those innards of yours. Where's your wife?'

'Gorn,' said Albert, in a whisper. 'For good.'

None of the three men tried to dispute the statement. The signs of a fight downstairs, the empty clothes cupboard in the bedroom, and the general disorder, were plain enough. There had been plenty of talk about the Piggotts' differences, and about the oil man's advances. Albert, they knew, was speaking the truth.

'We'd better let her know anyway,' said the doctor. 'Know her address?'

'No,' said Albert shortly. 'Nor want to.' He closed his eyes.

An hour later he was asleep between the sheets at Lulling Cottage Hospital, and Harold and Charles were telling Dimity what had happened.

'She's bound to come back,' she said. 'She wouldn't leave him just like that – not in hospital, not when she hears that he's ill!'

'I agree that most women would bury the hatchet when they heard that their husbands had been taken ill, but somehow,' said Harold, admiring his whisky against the light, 'I don't think Nelly will return in a hurry.'

'But what will he do?' asked the rector, looking distressed. 'He must have someone to look after him when he comes out of hospital!'

'I know,' said Dimity suddenly. 'I'll write to Molly, his daughter. She married Ben Curdle, the man who owns the fair,' she told Harold. 'She left here just before you came to live here. A dear girl – we all liked her so much. She should know anyway, and perhaps she will come and look after him.'

'He wasn't very nice to her when she did live with him,' ventured the rector doubtfully. 'And now she has Ben and the baby to look after, I really can't see – '

'Never mind,' said Dimity firmly. 'I shall let her know what has happened, and it is up to her to decide. I must ring Joan Young for her address. I know she keeps in touch. They were such friends when Molly used to be nursemaid to Paul.'

She made her way briskly to the study, and the two men heard her talking to Joan.

The rector gave a loud yawn and checked himself hastily.

'I'm so sorry. I'm unconscionably tired. It's the upset, I suppose. Poor Albert! I feel very distressed for him.'

'You'd feel distressed for Satan himself,' replied Harold affectionately. 'Poor Albert, indeed! I bet he asked for it. I don't blame Nelly for leaving that old devil.'

'I married them myself,' said the rector sadly, gazing at the fire. 'I must admit, I had doubts at the time.'

Dimity returned, a piece of paper fluttering in her hand.

'I've got the address. If I write now, then Willie can take it in the morning.'

'Well, I must be off,' said Harold rising. 'Many thanks for the drink.'

'I've just thought,' cried Dimity, standing transfixed. 'Did you see Albert's cat? I'd better go across and feed it.'

'You leave it till the morning,' advised Harold, patting her thin shoulder. 'It won't hurt tonight. There's plenty of Christmas pudding lying about the kitchen to keep it going.'

Signs of Christmas were beginning to appear in Lulling and Thrush Green.

The squat Butter Market cross, beloved by residents and antiquarians from further afield, was being wreathed in coils of wire ready for its garland of coloured lights later on.

In the shops, gifts were on display. Puddocks, the stationers, decked one of their windows with Christmas cards and the other with a fearsome array of table mats arranged round a scarlet typewriter. Ella found the juxtaposition of these articles extremely annoying, and said so to the manager.

'If you're going to show table mats put something like a large dish, or a vase with Christmas decorations in it,' Ella told him, in a voice audible to all his customers.

'Or if you want the ruddy typewriter on show – though who on earth you imagine is going to pay over thirty quid for one Christmas present these days, I'm blessed if I know – then put office stuff round it. Blotters, say, or calendars, or pens and pencils. But to mix up the two just isn't good enough!'

The manager made perfunctory apologies. As a young man he had dreaded Ella's comments. Now that he was grey and tubby he was hardened to this awkward customer's remarks. Ella Bembridge was a byword in the town. No one was going to worry about her little foibles, he told himself.

He directed her attention to the other window.

'I've done my own,' said Ella, scrutinizing the crinolined ladies, the churches in the snow, and the kittens in paper hats, with obvious disgust.

'Appalling, aren't they?' she said cheerfully, and departed before the manager could think of a cutting reply.

The window of the electricity showroom was much admired by the young if not by their elders. It showed an all-electric kitchen with the oven prominently displayed. The oven door

stood open, the better to show a dark-brown shiny turkey
and some misshapen roast potatoes. At the kitchen table, a
smiling woman stirred something which seemed to be Christmas pudding mixture, while a dish of mince-pies stood on the
top of the refrigerator beside her.

Quite rightly, the good wives of Lulling found this scene as
exasperating as Ella found Puddocks' window.

'Bit late mixin' the pudden,' one said sourly to another.

'And that bird won't get done with the door open,'
agreed her friend tartly. 'I shouldn't care to try them spuds
either.'

'Nor them mince-pies,' observed another. 'Plaster-a-Paris
as plain as a pike staff. Bet some fool of a man arranged that
window. I've a good mind to go in and tell 'em.'

'The Fuchsia Bush' had excelled itself with rows and rows
of silver bells, made from tinfoil, which were strung across
the ceiling and rustled metallically every time the door opened.

'Come in handy for keeping the birds off the peas later,'
observed one practical customer, speaking fortissimo above the
din of the dancing bells.

The bow-shaped windows were studded with dabs of
cotton-wool to represent snowflakes, and two imposing flower
arrangements of dried grasses, seed-pods and fern, all sprayed
with silver by the ladies of the Lulling Floral Society, took
pride of place in each window.

Thrush Green's preparations were less spectacular, but
Dimity took out the figures for the Christmas crib and washed
them carefully in luke-warm water well-laced with Lux.

Miss Watson and Miss Fogerty were in the throes of rehearsals for the annual Christmas concert. Miss Fogerty, who
was the more realistic of the two and knew the limits of her
infants' powers, had wisely plumped for simple carols, sung in
unison by the whole class, with 'growlers' tucked strategically
at the back of the stage and warned to 'sing very quietly'. A
few percussion instruments in the hands of the most competent
few, who included young Jeremy Prior, were going to ac-
company the infant choir.

In fact, Miss Fogerty's main concern was to get the children to pronounce their vowel sounds correctly. Constant repetition of:

> 'Awy in er-er mynger'

was causing her acute distress.

Miss Watson, who was more ambitious, had decided rashly to stage a nativity play. The ten-year-olds who were the most senior of her pupils and who, it might be supposed, would be competent to play the leading roles, were at the self-conscious stage, and tended to giggle and look sheepish, which Miss Watson found both irritating and irreligious.

She found herself speaking with unusual sharpness.

'Don't mumble into your beard, Joseph. The parents want to hear you, remember. And if you three wise men keep tripping over the rector's spare room curtains I shall be returning them in shreds. Pick your feet up, do! As for you beasts in the stall, for pity's sake stop nodding your masks in that inane way. You'll have them off, and I'm not made of cardboard!'

With such travail was Christmas being welcomed at the school.

'I suppose it will be all right on the day,' said Miss Watson resignedly to Miss Fogerty.

'Of course it will,' Miss Fogerty replied stoutly, watching her children paste paper chains with frenzied brushes, and more chatter than was usually allowed. She dived upon one five-year-old who was twirling his paste-brush energetically in his neighbour's ear, removed the brush, slapped the offender's hand, and lifted the malefactor to the corner where he was obliged to study the weather chart for December, with his back to the class. Throughout the whole incident, Miss Fogerty's face remained calm and kindly.

Miss Watson sighed. Dear Agnes's methods were hopelessly old-fashioned, and she knew quite well that corporal punishment was frowned upon by all enlightened educationalists.

Nevertheless, thought Miss Watson, returning to her own boisterous class, a sharp slap seemed to work wonders now and again, and at times, like this, one surely could be forgiven.

In the houses round the green, more preparations were going on. Ella had looked out half a dozen lumpy ties, ear-marked for male friends such as Charles Henstock. The Christmas cards, a stack of bold woodcuts with a certain rough attraction, waited on the dresser for despatch later.

Her present to Dimity remained to be finished. She was sewing a rug, in a stitch called 'tiedbrick stitch', in gay stripes of scarlet, grey and white. It gave her enormous satisfaction to do, but its bulk was difficult to hide in a hurry, on the occasions when Dimity called unexpectedly to see her.

Harold Shoosmith, efficient as ever, had bought book tokens for all his friends, and had a neat pile waiting in his desk to be written in, and posted on the correct day. Betty Bell had made him a Christmas pudding large enough for a family of ten, and was upset when her employer told her firmly that he refused to countenance her proposal to make him a dozen mince-pies, two trifles and a couple of jellies 'to keep him going'.

'My dear Betty,' he said kindly, 'I'm going to Christmas dinner with the rector and his wife. I have invited them here for Boxing Day evening, as you know, and that delicious Christmas pudding will be ample.'

'You'd best have a trifle as well,' said Betty mutinously. 'Miss Dimity likes trifle.'

'Very well,' sighed Harold capitulating. '*One trifle!* And thank you.'

Across the green, Phil Prior wrapped a few presents for Jeremy and hid them among her clothes, but her heart was not in the coming festivities. The prospect for her was bleak, and any day now she must steel herself to break the news to Jeremy that his father would not be there at Christmas time. The boy would have to know the truth before long. If only she could get it over!

Meanwhile, she worked hard at her writing, and prepared a batch of stories, articles and ideas, which might interest Frank when she met him for the first time on the Wednesday.

The day dawned clear and bright. Phil watched Jeremy eat his breakfast egg, and felt surprisingly excited by the prospect of a day in London.

'And I go straight to Aunt Joan's, don't I?' he said, for the third time. 'She's having sausages because I told her I liked them. Paul said so.'

'Then you're very lucky,' said his mother. 'Don't forget to thank her when you go back to school.'

'And you'll be back to put me to bed?'

'Of course. Probably by tea time, but it just depends how long I have to spend with the editor, and how the trains run.'

'Can't you come back with Richard?'

'No. He's staying in London.'

'D'you like him?' Jeremy's gaze was fixed upon her intently.

'Of course.' Jeremy drained his cup of milky coffee, and wiped away his wet moustache.

'I don't.'

'Why not? He's very kind. He cleared our drain for us, you know.'

'He did that for *you*,' said Jeremy shrewdly. 'Not for me. He doesn't notice me.'

Children! thought Phil, clearing the table swiftly. Too quick by half!

'Why should you mind that?' she answered reasonably. 'Grown-up people have a lot to think about. They don't always take notice of children.'

Jeremy made no reply, but bent to tie his shoelaces. This was a new accomplishment, and gave him great satisfaction.

'Miss Fogerty gave me two sweets the first time I tied my laces,' he said, surveying his shoes proudly.

'Two? Why two?' asked Phil, glad to have the subject changed.

'Dolly mixture,' replied her son briefly.

She helped him on with his coat, and gave him a hug. His soft face smelt sweetly of Morny pink lilac soap, as he kissed her.

'Have a lovely time,' he said cheerfully.

'You too,' said Phil, opening the front door. 'Have a lovely time,' she echoed, when he reached the gate.

She watched him run across the grass and turned back to

make her preparations, turning over in her mind the child's comments on their neighbour.

She enjoyed the drive with Richard. He was quick and competent in traffic, and quite unruffled by the antics of bad drivers around him.

They talked of Thrush Green, of books, and of music.

'There's a concert at Oxford just before Christmas,' said Richard. 'Will you come?'

'Thank you,' said Phil. 'If I can get someone to mind Jeremy, I should love to.'

'Aunt Winnie would sit-in, I'm sure,' said Richard. 'I'll ask her.'

'No, please don't. She's been so kind – '

'She's always kind. Looks after me too well,' said Richard, and began to tell her about his dietary difficulties.

For the first time, Phil began to see why Winnie Bailey found her nephew something of a trial. It seemed incredible that an intelligent grown man should be quite so worried about himself.

'But who is this Otto?' asked Phil, when the great man's name cropped up yet again.

'The wisest dietician of our time,' pronounced Richard solemnly, swerving to evade a cyclist bent on suicide. He went on to explain Otto's theories, his methods and his astounding successes. Phil did her best not to yawn.

'Where can I drop you?' asked Richard as they drove along Piccadilly. 'I have to go up Regent Street, if that's any help.'

'Yes, please. Somewhere near Hamley's if it's possible. I want to buy a gadget for Jeremy's train set.'

'Good luck with the editor,' called Richard, when she left the car. He gave her one of his disarming smiles, and Phil momentarily forgot the boredom of his digestive troubles as she thanked him and said good-bye.

The sausages were splendid – crisp and very dark brown – exactly as Jeremy and Paul liked them. As an added attraction, Joan had tucked them into an oblong of mashed potato with only the ends showing.

'Sausages-in-bed,' she told them. Jeremy was entranced with this gastronomic refinement, and determined to tell his mother how much better sausages tasted when so served.

The Youngs' ginger kitten greeted the boys affectionately.

'We're having one too,' Jeremy told Paul, proudly. 'It's coming at the weekend and I'm making a bed for it out of a cardboard box. I've got a piece of a rug to put at the bottom. A car rug my Daddy bought.'

'What's he giving you for Christmas?' asked Paul, a direct child.

'My daddy? I'm not sure.'

'He'll probably bring you a surprise,' said Paul.

'Yes,' agreed Jeremy. There was a slight doubtfulness in his tone which did not escape Joan, who knew the sad circumstances. 'If he comes,' he added thoughtfully.

'Of course he'll come,' scoffed Paul robustly. 'Bound to at Christmas.'

The school bell began to ring, and Joan held up a finger.

'A quick wash, Jeremy, and then off you go. We'll see you after school, my dear.'

Truly saved by the bell, she thought!

She spent the afternoon engaged in her own Christmas preparations. Her sister Ruth Lovell and her husband and baby were coming for Christmas Day. Her parents were arriving on Christmas Eve and would spend several days at Thrush Green. Mr Bassett, father of Joan and Ruth, had now retired, and was always threatening – in the kindest possible way – to turn out the Youngs from their Thrush Green house. It had been left to him on the death of his parents, and one day, he promised himself, he would go there to live.

She busied herself in preparing their room and sorting out bed-linen and blankets. The time passed so quickly that she was surprised to hear the shouts of the school children as they emerged at half past three.

She hurried downstairs to meet young Jeremy who was rushing up the garden path, unbelievably grubby after two hours in school.

'Let me wash your face,' she said, 'and then we'll go down to

Lulling to pick up Paul. And shall we buy some crumpets for tea?'

Sitting beside his hostess in the car Jeremy spoke decidedly.

'Next to my house,' he told her, 'I like yours best. If I hadn't got a home, could I live with you?'

'Anytime,' said Joan sincerely. 'Anytime, Jeremy.'

Travelling back alone, in the train, Phil closed her eyes and pondered on the day's happenings, well content.

She had liked Frank the moment she saw him. He was tall, heavily-built, with a beautiful deep voice and very bright eyes of that true brown which is so rare.

She found him remarkably easy to talk to, and found herself telling him far more about her circumstances than she intended, over a splendid lunch.

The work he had in mind, he told her, was similar to that which she already did for young girls. Would she be interested in writing a half page for a monthly for slightly younger children of both sexes? He told her the payment he had in mind, which was extremely generous.

'And more stories, please,' he said, 'for the women. I like your touch. Tell me more about the one you want me to suppress.'

She told him the details.

'Harold is far nicer than I am,' she admitted. 'I would have gone ahead, but it would have upset him, I'm sure.'

'He's a very fine chap,' said Frank. 'And most meticulous. But I can see no real reason why you should stand to lose your proper reward.'

He went on to tell her that his company owned two Scottish evening papers which printed a short story daily.

'No possible chance of Thrush Green eyes seeing them,' he told her. 'And we'll use a pseudonym. Think one up, and let me have it. I liked that tale. You handled the two old ladies beautifully.'

After lunch, they returned to the office where he gave her a number of back copies of the young people's magazine to study at home. They discussed things very thoroughly, and

Phil was surprised to find how quickly the time flew past.

'It's so good to be doing something again,' she said. 'You shall have the copy very quickly.'

'Tell Harold I will come and see him when Christmas is over. You will be spending it at home, I suppose?'

'Yes.'

'I'm going to my son's. He's farming in Wales and there are four children, under ten, so I shall be lively enough. It's rather flat being on one's own at Christmas. My boy Robert understands that.'

They wished each other good-bye and Phil set off for Paddington feeling happier than she had done for many a long day.

14. *Sudden Death*

WHEN Albert Piggott came round in hospital, he was bewildered and resentful. Where was his comfortable feather pillow, familiarly sour-smelling and crumpled? Where was the sides-to-middled sheet, soft with age? And worse still, where was the cane-bottomed chair beside the bed, with the glass for his teeth and his tin of extra strong peppermints?

Everything was wrong. The light was too bright. The ceiling was too clean and too far away. And now that he could focus his aching eyes, why were there other beds around him?

He tried to sit up, but a pain in his head felled him like a log. After a little while, he managed to turn his head on the hard starched pillow and surveyed the occupant of the next bed through half-shut eyes. Outlined against the bright window, the man appeared simply as a dark hulk to Albert, but he was aware that he was being watched closely.

'Comin' round then, Bert?' he said kindly, and Albert's heart sank still further. If it wasn't Ted Allen, who kept 'The Drovers' Arms' at Lulling Woods! And could he talk? Just his luck to be beside an old gas-bag like Ted Allen! Albert shut his eyes tightly.

'Nurse!' shouted Ted, in a bellow that set Albert's head throbbing. 'Mr Piggott's come round. Looks a bit poorly.'

He felt a cool hand on his hot forehead, and another hand holding his wrist. He opened one eye – the one furthest from Ted Allen – with extreme caution.

A fresh-faced young girl smiled down at him beneath her starched cap.

'Feeling better now?' she asked.

'No,' said Albert.

'Like a drink?'

'What of?' asked Albert, with a flicker of interest.

'Water? Cold milk?'

'No thanks,' said Albert disgustedly.

'He could do with a pint of bitter, nurse,' said Ted with hearty jocularity.

Albert winced.

'Now, Mr Allen,' said the nurse severely, 'don't be a tease. Mr Piggott needs his rest. I'm going to put a screen round his bed for an hour or two.'

'Thank God for that,' said Albert, and meant it.

Later, after some hours of fitful dozing, the nurse came back, removed the screen, and lifted him against the pillows.

'Like some supper?' she said brightly.

'What is it?' asked Albert suspiciously.

'You'll see,' said the nurse, with an archness that annoyed Albert.

She whisked away. Bet it wouldn't be anything as good as Nelly cooked him, he thought morosely.

Nelly! What was it about Nelly, that he ought to remember? Something to do with Christmas pudding and shouting and a row. He groaned with the effort of thinking.

'You all right, old chap? Anything I can do?' asked Ted solicitously.

'Shut yer gob,' said Albert rudely.

'Thanks, I'm sure,' said Ted, offended. Blessed silence fell, and Albert tried out his powers of memory again.

Nelly shouting at him. Banging down a suitcase on the table. The oilman! Now he'd got it!

She'd gone!

With horror, Albert found his eyes were wet. Within a minute two tears were rolling down his cheeks. What had come over him? He was damned if he was crying about Nelly, he told himself fiercely. Good riddance to bad rubbish, that was! Nothing but everlasting rows and nagging ever since she'd caught him!

Too proud to wipe the tears away with Ted's sharp eyes upon him, Albert watched the tears splash down upon the snowy sheet top, making neat round stains.

The nurse came back bearing a small bowl full of some milky substance.

'Now, now, now!' she scolded him. 'What are we getting upset about?'

She whisked a paper tissue from a box nearby and mopped Albert's face painfully.

'Upsadaisy now!' she said, heaving him a little higher in the bed. 'Cheer up, cheer up! Worse troubles at sea! Have some supper. That'll put new heart into us.'

Albert surveyed the contents of the bowl sourly.

'Don't eat slops,' he said flatly.

'It's all you're going to get for a bit,' said the nurse firmly, 'so you may as well get used to it.'

'Why?' asked Albert, with some spirit. 'What's up with me? What you been doin' to me while I was unconscious?'

'You've had an operation for a very nasty ulcer,' said the nurse primly.

'Bin *cut*, 'ave I?' yelped Albert, outraged.

'Our Mr Pedder-Bennett performed the operation,' said the girl reverently. 'A beautiful bit of work, the theatre sister said.'

'That ol' butcher?' cried Albert indignantly. I'll have the law on the lot of you! Letting that ol' saw-bones loose on a chap as is unconscious. I'll—'

'You'll eat your supper,' said the nurse, deftly thrusting a spoonful into Albert's protesting mouth. 'And stop talking nonsense.'

She lodged the bowl in front of him and bustled out of the ward.

Albert removed the spoon from his mouth and pushed it about in the bowl gloomily. He became conscious of other people eating in the ward, and looked at his companions with some interest.

Ted Allen kept his eyes sedulously upon his tray. His expression was lofty. He wasn't going to waste his time being pleasant to an old misery like Albert Piggott. Let him stew in his own juice!

'What've they given you?' asked Albert, trying to make amends. Ted Allen, good-hearted, quickly forgave his neighbour.

'Some sort of mince,' said Ted. 'Could be anything from rat to rabbit. You name it – this is it!'

'Looks a sight better than this muck,' said Albert, with considerable self-pity.

'You wants to take things careful,' advised Ted. 'You was pretty bad when you come in. And a proper ghastly colour when they brought you back from the operation. Lay there groaning, you did, and snoring horrible.'

'Did I now?' said Albert, brightening. 'Bet you thought I wouldn't come round.'

'That never worried us,' said Ted ambiguously. 'But you kep' us all awake.'

Albert tried another spoonful tentatively and pondered Ted's last remark.

'What you in for?' he asked at length.

'Appendix. Caught me while I was lifting the crates. Good thing Bessie was nearby. She got Doctor Lovell double quick and here we are. I goes out sometime this week.'

'You're lucky,' growled Albert.

Ted Allen looked about him reflectively.

'I don't know. I've quite enjoyed meself, being waited on. Makes a nice change. And people comin' to see you with fruit and papers. I'll be quite sorry to go, what with one thing and another.'

'Don't suppose anyone'll come and see me,' said Albert.

'What about Nelly? She'll be down with a steak-and-kidney pud hidden in her pocket, I'll bet.'

'That she won't,' replied Albert, putting the spoon and bowl on the locker top. 'She's cleared off!' No point in trying to keep secrets in Lulling, he told himself.

'You don't say!' gasped Ted, registering acute surprise. Bessie had told him the news twenty-four hours earlier. She had also told him about the oilman. 'What did she do that for?'

'Gone off her chump over some fellow that's no better than he should be,' replied Albert austerely. 'That's why.'

'She's a fool then,' said Ted. 'Throwing over a steady chap like you.'

Albert looked mollified. There was one thing about Ted Allen, blab-mouth though he was. He was a good judge of character, thought Albert.

The nurse came scurrying down to his bed, and peered into his bowl.

'That's better. Next time you must finish it all up, but we'll let you off tonight. Feeling happier now, are we?'

'No,' said Albert.

'Well, you will when I tell you the news,' said the girl, undeterred. 'Your daughter's here to see you.'

'What? Molly?'

'Yes, and her husband. Now, you be nice to them. They've come a long way.'

She beckoned to two figures at the end of the ward. They advanced shyly. For one terrible minute, Albert thought that the tears would come again. Weakness it was, just weakness, he told himself, fighting for control.

'Dad,' said Molly. 'How are you feeling now?'

'Middlin',' said Albert huskily. She put a small posy of anemones on the bed.

'They must have cost a pretty penny,' commented Albert ungratefully.

'Never mind that,' said Ben. 'You look better than I thought you would.'

'Been at death's door, I have,' Albert said with pride. 'Ain't I, Ted?'

'Mr Allen!' cried Molly, turning round. 'And how's your wife, and "The Drovers' Arms"? Those were happy times!'

They talked for a minute or two, for they were old friends. Molly had worked there as barmaid before her marriage, and the Allens had always been good to her.

'You heard about Nelly?' asked Albert.

'Yes, dad. Miss Dimity told me when we got here. I'm sorry. What'll you do?'

'Same as I did before, of course. Look after meself. I ain't helpless, you know.'

'We know that,' said Ben diplomatically. 'But best see how you get over this operation. Maybe, Molly can look after you for a bit until you're on your legs again. I can spare her for a week or two.'

The two young people smiled at each other. It was plain to Albert that they had been making plans before they paid this visit.

Suddenly, he felt ineffably tired. It had been a long day. Seeing the look of exhaustion, Molly rose and nudged Ben.

'We'll be off now, Dad, and come and see you tomorrow before we go back home.'

She kissed his unresponsive face. Ben shook his hand gently, and they departed.

'She's a grand girl,' said Ted Allen, watching them go. 'Always bright and cheerful, as Bessie says.'

'Takes after her old dad,' said Albert drowsily, and fell into a deep sleep.

In the week that followed Phil's trip to town, she worked hard at the writing. It was always difficult to begin a new type of work, and she had never written for children of ten to fourteen for whom the new column was intended.

Nevertheless, she had experience with slightly older readers, and she was comforted by the thought that Frank was the sort of person who would say exactly what was right, or wrong, with a piece of work, and also give her sound advice.

She had passed on his message to Harold who looked pleased at the thought of entertaining his old friend.

'And I think I ought to tell you,' she added, after some hesitation, 'that the story about the two village ladies is to be published after all.'

She explained about the Scottish papers and the pen-name. Harold was elated.

'I'm so glad. I've felt rather wretched over the whole affair. I'm afraid you must have thought me unspeakably stuffy.'

'Well, I was horribly rude. I was so cross,' laughed Phil. 'Still, all's well that ends well, and I really am most terribly grateful to you for introducing me to Frank and all this lovely work. I shall be quite rich in the New Year.'

The next morning, while Phil was tapping busily at her

typewriter, Harold appeared at the window, waving a pair of secateurs.

'Would you like me to prune those roses at the end of the garden? We missed them earlier, you remember. I've just finished mine, and thought I'd ask while it was in my mind.'

'I'd be very thankful,' said Phil, 'I'm particularly dim about pruning. I'll give you a call when I'm making coffee. I just want to finish some alterations.'

'Don't disturb yourself on my account,' said Harold cheerfully, departing down the garden.

It was a clear mild December day. Against the house, a flourishing winter jasmine was breaking into yellow stars. A robin eyed Harold speculatively from the top of the wall, hoping for upturned worms. Nearby, a fat thrush jabbed rhythmically at a rotting apple in the grass.

Harold got on with the job, humming happily to himself. It was a relief to know that all was well between himself and Phil, and an even greater relief to know that she was getting steady work which was decently rewarded.

He was making a neat job of the neglected bushes, and stacking the prickly shoots in a pile ready for burning, when he heard the gate click, and looked up.

Stepping up the path was the local policeman, Constable Potter. He hailed him gaily. The officer walked across the grass towards him.

'And what brings you here?' asked Harold lightly. 'Traffic offences?'

The constable remained unsmiling, and Harold felt a sudden constriction in his chest.

'Not bad news, I hope?'

'Afraid so, sir. But I must tell Mrs Prior first. Is she alone, d'you know?'

'Yes. The boy's at school. But can I help?'

'Not yet, sir. But will you be around?'

'Yes, of course. I'll be here, in the garden.'

He watched the burly blue back advance towards Tullivers' front door with heavy foreboding.

For Harold, there followed the longest ten minutes he could

remember. Mechanically he snipped at the rose bushes, while the robin whistled to him. He collected handfuls of dried grass which were caught about the lower shoots like grey lace, and added them, unseeing, to his pile of rubbish. What could have happened? Was it something to do with the divorce? Wouldn't her solicitor cope with all that? Why on earth would young Potter want to call?

At length, the front door opened and the two emerged. Constable Potter replaced his cap, and made his farewells in a low voice. He gave one swift anxious look in Harold's direction, raised a hand, and stumped heavily down the path.

Phil, looking pale and stunned, walked across the grass to Harold who hurried towards her. She looked ready to faint, but when she reached him she held up her arms like a bewildered child and clung to him.

'There, there,' Harold heard himself say, as he patted her back. 'Come into the house, my love, and tell me.'

They entered the house, hand in hand, and in silence. When he had settled her in an armchair, he stood waiting, his back to the fire.

'Brandy?' he asked gently.

She shook her head. At last she spoke.

'I can't believe it. He's dead.'

She raised her eyes slowly, and looked mutely at Harold.

'That policeman. He brought a message from Paris. John's been killed in his car.'

'Oh no!' whispered Harold. 'This is terrible news. Terrible!'

'I must go. I must get over there.' She rose unsteadily and leant against the mantelpiece.

'I told the policeman I must go. He left a piece of paper with the times of the flights.'

She began to wander distractedly about the room, searching in an aimless way. Harold saw a piece of paper protruding from her cardigan pocket. He took it out and studied it.

'The next one is at two o'clock,' he told her. 'Let me take you over this afternoon.'

'No, no!' The girl faced him more steadily.

'I'd sooner go alone. I must go alone on this journey.'

'Then let me take you up to Heathrow.'

'I'd be grateful for that. I'll go and get some things together.'
She stopped suddenly.

'But Jeremy? I must arrange something for Jeremy.'

'I'll take charge of that,' said Harold. 'I'll call and see Joan
Young, and go and get the car, while you pack.'

He looked at her white face anxiously.

'Have that drop of brandy before you begin,' he said. She
nodded, and he fetched her a tot in a glass, standing over her
while she gulped it down, shuddering.

'I'll be back in a quarter of an hour,' he told her. 'Wrap up
well, and don't forget your passport.'

She nodded again, dumbly, and he hurried across the green
on his errands. Still dry-eyed, Phil went upstairs very slowly,
like an old, old woman, to prepare for the saddest journey of
her life.

She scarcely spoke on the way to the airport but sat with
her hands clenched tightly upon the handbag in her lap.

They had some time to wait and Harold fetched coffee and
sandwiches as they sat in the crowded waiting room.

Beside Phil sat two women with the most clownish make-up
that Harold had ever encountered. He found his eyes straying
to the green eyelids, the black-rimmed eyes, and the curiously
luminous lips. His father would have made no bones about
labelling them 'strumpets', thought Harold, but apart from
their outlandish faces, they seemed normal enough. Their dress
was plain, their speech quiet, their apologies sincere when they
accidentally jogged Phil's coffee-cup. Harold was baffled.

The food seemed to revive Phil. She smiled tremulously at
him, as though she were seeing him for the first time.

'I can never thank you enough for today,' she told him
softly. 'You understand how I feel about going to John alone,
though?'

'Of course,' he told her.

'I don't really believe it's happened,' she said wonderingly.
'I don't want to cry, because I just don't believe it.'

She turned to him suddenly.

'Look after Jeremy, won't you? Tell Joan what's happened. I'll tell Jeremy later.'

He patted her arm comfortingly.

'Are you all right for money?' he asked.

'I've a cheque book, and about five pounds.'

He took out his wallet and gave her some notes.

'It's simpler to have ready money. You don't know what expenses you'll find. If you want me to come over, just ring. I'm absolutely free to come at any hour, as you know.'

'I'll remember.'

'And I'll meet you here, in any case.'

'Dear Harold,' said Phil softly.

A booming voice above, nasal and distorted, announced that passengers for the flight must now depart. Phil rose hurriedly, and went with Harold to the door.

'Don't wait, please,' she told him. 'You've done so much. Get back to dear Thrush Green.'

She was swallowed up in the crowd of travellers and vanished from his sight.

But Harold did not return to Thrush Green until he had gone to the roof of the building and watched the plane take off. He watched until its greyness merged into the greyness of the December sky, before turning to go home.

15. *Harold Takes Charge*

THE departure of Nelly Piggott from Thrush Green may not have upset her husband unduly, but it certainly distressed Miss Watson and Miss Fogerty.

Every morning and evening Nelly had cleaned Thrush Green school with all the vigour of her thirteen stone. The classrooms, lobbies, windows – even the dingy old map-cupboard – were kept spotless. Nor had Nelly chided the children for stepping in snow or mud.

'So good-hearted,' mourned Miss Watson. 'And so *thorough*.' She lowered her voice.

'Did you know, Agnes, that she scoured the outside drains every morning? Scrupulously clean – scrupulously!'

'I can't think how poor Albert Piggott will manage without her,' said Miss Fogerty compassionately. 'He'll need someone there when he comes out of hospital.'

'Well now,' began Miss Watson, looking important, 'I heard a rumour that Molly might be back for a bit.'

'Splendid!' cried Miss Fogerty, clapping her small hands together. 'Dear Molly!'

'It's not *definite*, Agnes dear,' said Miss Watson severely. 'Don't repeat it, until we've had it confirmed. As you know, I cannot abide idle gossip. But certainly, that's what I heard.'

'I shan't breathe a word,' promised Miss Fogerty solemnly. 'But I do so hope you heard aright.'

She turned her attention to the hymn book in her hand.

'What shall we have this morning?' she asked her head-mistress. '"Jesus bids us shine"?'

'I am afraid it had better be a carol, dear. They still need plenty of practice before the concert. "Away in a manger", perhaps?'

Miss Fogerty winced.

'Not again, please. I have to go through it so often.'

'Very well,' said Miss Watson indulgently. 'You choose, Agnes dear.'

'What about "Once in royal"?'

'Splendid,' said Miss Watson, looking about for a bell-ringer. Her eye lit upon Ben Lane who was engrossed in cleaning the doorknob with a spat-upon handkerchief.

'You may ring the bell, dear,' she said graciously. A tag from her well-worn college notes came into her mind.

'Always direct the child's energies into useful channels.'

Of course, she thought, a minute later, as the school bell rang out its warning to late-comers, we may need the children's labour to keep the school clean now that Nelly's gone. But Ben Lane's methods, of course, *would not* be countenanced.

Nothing had been heard from the departed lady. The oilman had left Lulling without giving anyone an address, so that neighbours put two and two together, as always, and this time came to the right conclusion. The love-birds had flown together.

The local paper had Albert Piggott's story in it. Not, of course, the story of his broken marriage, but a sensational one about his dramatic collapse.

'St Andrew's Sexton Found Unconscious' it said boldly. And in smaller print below: 'Timely Aid by Vicar.'

'I do wish,' said Charles Henstock, quite waspishly for such a kindly man, 'that papers would get their facts right. Everyone here knows I'm a *rector*.' He read the rest of the story with an expression of marked distaste on his chubby countenance, but his comment was typically Christian.

'Perhaps Nelly will see this, wherever she is, and come back to him.'

'More fool her if she does,' said Ella who was present.

She voiced the general sentiments of Thrush Green.

But the drama of the Piggotts was soon overshadowed by Phil Prior's sad news. Despite the fact that her husband seemed to be 'a proper fast one', as they had observed to each other, Thrush Green folk were sincerely shocked by the tragedy which had befallen the newcomer, who had so quickly become one of the community.

Harold Shoosmith, on his return, had gone at once to see Joan Young. The little boys were playing in the garden with Flo, the old spaniel, and he could speak openly.

'She's in a pretty bad state of shock, naturally,' he said, 'but wanted to go through this business alone. She'll ring tomorrow to let us know what's happening. I've told her to telephone me. I hope you don't mind? I'm there alone, and it might be awkward for you if the boys were within earshot.'

'By far the best thing,' agreed Joan. 'I hope she won't feel that she must hurry to get back to Jeremy – though I know she'll want to, of course. But he's a dear child, and fits in so happily.'

'There'll be a few formalities to go through, no doubt, but I should think she'll be back in about two or three days. It depends on the funeral arrangements.'

He walked to the window and stood staring across the chestnut avenue to the green. Joan could see how worried he was and, woman-like, knew why without being told.

'Would you like to come and have dinner here tonight with us?' she asked impulsively. 'Edward and I would love it, if you are free.'

As though he knew what was in her mind, he turned quickly and smiled.

'You're very kind, but I ought to write a letter or two, and I want to let the Baileys know about this. Winnie will wonder what's happened when she sees the house in darkness.'

'I understand,' said Joan.

A little later she saw him crossing to the doctor's house, and thought what an attractive man he was.

'Phil could do a lot worse,' she thought, then chided herself for thinking of such things, when poor John Prior was not yet in his grave.

Jeremy had asked only a few questions about his mother's absence, for which Joan was truly thankful.

'Why has she gone to France? To see Daddy?'

'Yes,' said Joan.

'Why so quickly? Why didn't she take me?'

'Daddy had an accident in the car, so she went straight away.'

'He always drives fast,' said Jeremy, proudly. 'Once we did *ninety*: *Ninety*!' he repeated.

'My uncle,' said Paul, 'once did a hundred and thirty. And my friend Chris says his father did *two hundred* on a straight road in Norfolk!'

'Don't boast,' said Joan. But she was glad to have had the subject changed, nevertheless.

Harold found the Baileys, and Richard, taking their ease and watching, in a lack-lustre way, a programme on television. Winnie rose to switch it off as he entered.

'Oh please, don't let me interrupt anything you want to see,' cried Harold.

'It's a relief to switch it off,' said the doctor. 'We've been too idle to do so. It's one of those tiresome interviews where the interviewer is obsessed with the importance of prepositions. You know the sort of thing – "The Minister is here, AT this moment to answer questions ON our policy IN regard TO our commitments." Dreadful stuff!'

'I'm so glad you've come in,' said Winnie. 'I was going to ask you about the garden next door. Do you think there is room for a rose bush or two? We thought we might give Phil a couple for Christmas.'

Harold looked at her quickly, and then at the doctor.

'Yes, I'm sure there's room for the roses. A lovely idea. As a matter of fact, it's Phil I've come about.'

He stopped, and the doctor thought how unusually exhausted he seemed.

'Richard, get us all a drink, there's a good fellow. Sherry, or whisky?'

'Sherry, please,' said Harold. He sat in silence while Richard handed glasses, and then began again.

'I'm afraid she's had bad news of her husband.'

'The divorce is through?' Winnie looked puzzled.

'No. He's had a car crash. In France.'

'Dead, I suppose,' said the doctor quietly.

Harold nodded.

'Poor, poor girl!' said Winnie, her face puckered with distress. 'I must go round at once.'

'No,' said Harold, 'that's what I came to tell you. She's over there already.'

'On her own?' said Richard sharply. 'Surely not on her own.'

'She preferred it that way,' Harold replied.

'Did she fly?'

'Yes. I took her to Heathrow this morning.'

'I'll meet her when she returns,' said Richard. 'I don't like the idea of her being alone through an ordeal like this. I wish I'd known earlier.'

Harold felt some irritation at Richard's assumption that his presence was necessary to Phil's well-being, but he tried to speak calmly.

'The arrangements are settled about her return,' he said. 'Of course, no one knows yet which day it will be.'

'I can be free at any time,' said Richard. Harold decided to ignore the remark, and turned to Winnie.

'Joan is taking care of Jeremy. He seems very cheerful there, and doesn't know the truth yet, of course.'

Doctor Bailey turned his glass thoughtfully round and round in his thin old hands.

'It is a dreadful affair. A young fellow like that. In his thirties, I suppose. She will be badly shaken, despite these last few months of separation.'

He looked up at Harold.

'What about the practical side? This must mean the end of her allowance from him. Is there anything to leave, do you know?'

'I've no idea. They probably hadn't much between them. After all, they haven't been married very long – not long enough to amass much in the way of savings.'

'What about her writing?'

'Chicken feed, I should think,' interjected Richard, who was now walking about, hands in pockets, looking extremely agitated.

'How I wish she had parents to turn to!' cried Winnie. 'She's so alone in the world.'

It was the feeling which was uppermost too in Harold's mind, but he felt unable to speak about it at the moment.

'I thought you should know the news,' he said, rising to go. 'Do you have a key to Tullivers, by any chance? I thought I might go round the house and make sure the switches are off, and the windows closed, and so on. We left pretty hurriedly.'

'I know where one is hidden,' said Winnie. Country folk invariably know where 'the secret key' is kept by their neighbours. On occasions such as this, it is a useful piece of knowledge.

'It's in the garden shed,' continued Winnie, 'on the ledge on the right hand side of the door, by the plant labels.'

'Good,' said Harold, 'I'll go and see to it now before it gets dark.'

'I'll come with you,' said Richard.

There was no earthly reason why he should be prevented, so that the two men walked together through the chilly dusk to Tullivers.

'My God,' said Richard. 'This is a fine thing! How will she manage? D'you think she'll move?'

'I've no idea. I don't think she'll want to.'

They plodded across the grass to the little shed which housed Phil's splendid new mower and the few poor broken tools which had distressed Harold by their uselessness. The key was carefully lodged behind the packet of plant labels, and they made their way to the front door.

Apart from a bathroom heater which had been left on, and a tap dripping at the kitchen sink, everything was in order. The scent of freesias hung about Phil's bedroom, bringing memories of her sharply to Harold.

'I know they didn't get on,' Richard said, as they descended the stairs, 'but this is a real blow for her. So dam' final, death, isn't it?'

Harold made a noise of agreement. Richard's obvious agitation was surprising. He had not met the fellow very often, and had no idea that he knew Phil as well as this concern for her seemed to show. Harold found his anxiety a trifle alarming.

'We can't do anything yet,' he observed reasonably. 'We

know nothing. One thing, she's a girl with plenty of courage and good sense. I'm sure she'll do nothing silly, or in a hurry.'

'She'll need advice,' said Richard.

'I understand she has a good solicitor,' replied Harold shortly.

He locked the front door, and put the key in his pocket. He intended to be the one to take charge of Tullivers while its owner was absent.

'If you'll excuse me,' he said politely, to Richard at the gate, 'I must get back.'

He set off homeward at a brisk pace, turning over this new development in Phil's affairs in his mind.

'And to think,' he said to himself as he opened his front door, 'that I chose to come to Thrush Green for a simple life!'

Winnie Bailey was taking coffee with Ella Bembridge the next morning when Dotty arrived bearing a large bundle of magazines, and the daily pint of goat's milk for Ella.

Thrush Green had a very sensible institution, started in wartime, called the magazine club. A number of residents each took a weekly or monthly magazine. They were collected together by one of the members and passed round in turn. In this way everyone saw a dozen or so journals regularly for the price of one. The rota had remained the same for years, only removals, or deaths, altering the system.

Ella took *Punch* although, as she said: 'It ceased to be funny after 1920.' The Baileys took *Country Life,* Harold *The Field,* Charles Henstock *The Church Times,* the Youngs weighed in with the *Spectator* and *The Listener* and Dotty contributed *The Lady* and *History Today.* Less intellectual matter was supplied by Ruth Lovell and various ladies at Lulling, and included 'really readable stuff', according to Dimity, who was no highbrow, such as *Woman, Woman's Own* and *Homes and Gardens.* It was interesting to note that these last three magazines were always the most well-thumbed when they came to be passed on. *The Field, The Church Times* and the *Spectator* remained immaculate for quite a time.

'Heard the news?' enquired Dotty, unwinding a long scarf

from her stringy neck, and dropping the bundle of magazines in the process.

The ladies bent down to put the bundle together again, Dotty uttering little cries of self-reproach the while.

'No harm done,' said Ella, straightening up. 'Have some coffee, Dot?'

'Thank you. I must say I was very surprised to hear about it.'

'About what?' asked Winnie carefully. She had just told Ella the sad news about John Prior, but had not realized that it might have reached as far as Lulling Woods already.

'A very good thing really,' continued Dotty. 'It had to come some time.'

'How d'you mean?' asked Winnie cautiously.

'Well, I mean, we're all getting older every day. Can't expect to carry on for ever. Taking the long view we'll all be the better for it.'

'What on earth,' said Ella downrightly, 'are you maundering on about, Dotty?'

Dotty looked hurt.

'Albert Piggott, of course. His wife's gone off with the oil-man, though how she could I just don't know. Such a vulgar fellow. Always talking about "the ladies", and "the fair sex", and "being a mere male". If it weren't for the fact that he comes right to the house with the paraffin, and carries very good old-fashioned wax tapers, I shouldn't allow him to call. Father would have shown him the door.'

'Yes, we had heard,' said Winnie. There was an ominous hissing sound from the kitchen.

'Blast! The milk!' cried Ella, stumping off.

'I'm having mine black just now,' Dotty informed her when she returned.

Ella, speechless for once, exchanged a meaning glance with Winnie.

'And had you heard that Molly may be coming back?' asked Dotty. 'I do so hope that she and that nice Curdle boy settle here. Did you know that she taught him to read and write after they were married? He didn't have much schooling, shifting about with the fair. I thought it was so clever of her to do that.'

'And brave of him to try,' agreed Winnie. 'Some men would have been too self-conscious to admit their ignorance.'

The ladies sipped their coffee and Winnie was about to let Dotty know Phil Prior's news when Dotty herself mentioned the girl.

'I'm taking the last of the kittens to Tullivers this weekend. I must say I shall miss them sorely. They've all turned out remarkably well-behaved and intelligent. How's Tabitha doing?'

Dimity and Charles had chosen the tabby with exceptionally fine eyes. Dotty kept a vigilant eye and ear open for news of the various kittens.

'Scoffing down ox liver at four-and-six a pound,' said Ella, 'last time I saw her.'

'Oh, I do so hope dear Dimity isn't over-doing the protein,' cried Dotty. 'A little raw liver is *excellent*, of course, but too much can be rather heating. I must have a word with her.'

She rose to make her departure. Winnie got up too. This seemed the time to break the news.

'I should leave the kitten for a little longer,' said Winnie. 'Phil Prior is away for a few days. In France, in fact.'

'At this time of year?' protested Dotty. 'If anything, the weather's worse than in England.'

'It's no pleasure trip,' Winnie said gravely. 'Her husband had an accident there. I'm sorry to say he has died. She's gone over to see about things.'

Dotty stood transfixed for a moment at the enormity of the news.

When she spoke, it was with her usual breathtaking directness.

'Sad, of course,' said Dotty, picking up the disreputable scarf, 'but it simplifies things a lot. Harold Shoosmith will be able to go ahead now, won't he?'

She preceded a stunned Winnie Bailey to the door, thanked Ella for the coffee, and bustled away down the path, her skinny legs, in their thick speckled stockings, twinkling energetically.

'Sometimes,' said Winnie faintly, 'I wonder if Dotty is clairvoyant.'

'She's an old witch,' responded Ella roundly.

20. *Harold Thinks Things Out*

PHIL PRIOR was away for four days. She rang Harold and Joan on alternate evenings and was mightily relieved to hear how little Jeremy appeared to miss her.

Everyone was being incredibly kind and helpful, she told them. Formalities had been hurried through, and she would return immediately after the funeral. John's parents had met her out there, and they were doing their best to comfort each other. Her plane was due to arrive at five-thirty, and she was longing to get back to the haven of Thrush Green and all her friends.

During her absence, Harold had plenty of time for thought. This tragedy had quickened his affection and admiration for the girl, and his determination to do all in his power to help her. Whether, in the distant future when she had recovered from the blow, she could ever contemplate marriage again, he had no idea. Whether he himself really wanted to give up his serene bachelorhood, he was not sure. But one thing he did know – if he ever should marry, then the only person he wanted was Phil.

He took several long solitary walks in the few days of Phil's absence, trying to come to terms with this new surprising feeling which so strangely moved him. The weather was mild and quiet, overcast and vaguely depressing, as though the world were in waiting for some momentous happening. Away from the domestic bustle of Christmas, the countryside was infinitely soothing, Harold found.

He found himself noting things with newly-awakened observation and sensibility. Tiny spears of snowdrop leaves were pushing through. Already the honeysuckle showed minute leafy rosettes, and in the still morning air, a thousand droplets quivered on the spikes of the hawthorn hedge.

Percy Hodge's black and white cows gazed at him over the gate, their long eyelashes rimed with mist, their sweet breath forming clouds in the quiet air. A thrush, head cocked side-ways, listened intently to the moving of a mole just beneath the surface of the grass verge. In Lulling Woods the trees dripped gently, their trunks striped with moisture, while underfoot the damp leaves deadened every footfall.

He returned from these lonely walks much refreshed in spirit, even if any sort of decision still evaded him. It was good to escape from people, now and again, and a positive relief to be away from Betty Bell's boisterous activities. The coming of Christmas seemed to rouse her to even greater energy, and carpets were beaten within an inch of their lives, pillows shaken until the feathers began to escape, paint was washed, windows polished and all to the accompaniment of joyful singing which Harold had not the heart to suppress.

'Got all your presents tied up?' asked Betty, busily winding up the Hoover cord into an intricate figure-of-eight arrange-ment, which Harold detested. It was useless to tell her that this was a strain on the covering of the cord cable. Figures-of-eight Betty Bell had always done, and would continue to do until her hand grew too frail to push the Hoover. Harold averted his eyes from the operation.

'Yes, Betty. I think everything's ready.'

'Want a Christmas tree?'

'No thanks.'

'Holly? Ivy? Anythink o' that?'

'Well, perhaps a little holly—'

'Fine. I'll send the kids out. Don't want to waste good money in the market, do you?'

'No,' agreed Harold. 'But only a sprig or two, Betty, please. I can't cope with a lot of stuff.'

'I'll see you right,' Betty assured him, flickering his desk energetically, and knocking his fountain pen to the floor. Harold retrieved it patiently.

'I suppose there's nothing 'eard from that Nelly Tilling? Piggott, I should say.'

'Not as far as I know.'

'Miss Watson's in a fine old taking,' said Betty conversa-tionally. 'Talking of getting that Mrs Cooke back as lives up

Nidden way. Must be hard up to want her to take over the school cleaning. Proper slummocky ha'porth, she is. Ever seen her?'

'I don't think so.'

'Once seen never forgotten.' Betty burst into a peal of laughter, as she picked up the Hoover, ready to depart to the kitchen. 'Ugly as sin, and could do with a good wash. You wouldn't fancy anything as she'd cooked, I can tell you. Ham omelette do you?'

'Beautifully,' said Harold. She bore away the Hoover, and slammed the study door with such vigour that it set a silver vase ringing on the mantelpiece.

Harold wandered to the window and looked out upon empty Thrush Green and the quiet countryside beyond. The lines of a hymn floated into his mind.

> Where every prospect please
> And only man is vile

Perhaps not 'vile', Harold thought forgivingly, but distracting certainly.

Two days before Albert Piggott's release from hospital, Molly Curdle arrived at her old home with her little son, George, an energetic toddler.

Ben, who had brought her, was obliged to return to his work, but promised to spend Sunday with his family. It was the first time the couple had been parted since their marriage, and Molly felt forlorn as she watched him drive away.

However, there was plenty to do at the neglected cottage, and she set to with her customary vigour. In the afternoon she was delighted to receive a visit from Joan Young, who was bearing a pretty little Christmas decoration of holly, Christmas roses and variegated ivy, set in a mossy base.

The two young women greeted each other affectionately, and George was admired by Joan, as much as the posy was admired by Molly.

'I can't tell you how lovely it is to have you back,' said Joan sincerely. 'How long can you stop?'

'Well, Ben and I hope it won't be for longer than a fortnight, but it depends on Dad. You know what he's like. He'd sooner manage on his own, I know, but he can't do that just yet.'

'No news of Nelly?'

'None. But she won't show up again, I'm positive. And frankly, I don't blame her. We never thought it would last.'

'Bring George to tea tomorrow,' said Joan. 'Paul's longing to see you and to show you off to his new friend Jeremy.'

Molly agreed with pleasure. She had always loved the Youngs' house, and had been very happy working there. She had learnt a great deal about managing children from looking after Paul as a young child, and this experience was standing her in good stead in bringing up George.

The tea party was much enjoyed. There was a rapturous reunion between Paul and Molly, and George enjoyed being the centre of attention. It was the last day of Molly's freedom, for the next morning her father arrived from the hospital and was put comfortably to bed.

She had expected him to be a demanding patient, but was surprised by his docility. Hospital discipline seemed to have improved Albert's manners. At times he was almost grateful for Molly's attentions. It couldn't last for ever, Molly told herself philosophically, but while it did, she enjoyed this rare spell of good behaviour.

His first short walk was across to St Andrew's church. It was not being cared for in the way he thought proper, as he pointed out to the rector when he called, but nevertheless he admitted grudgingly that it could be a lot worse. This was high praise indeed, from Albert, and the rector was suitably impressed.

'I really feel that affliction has mellowed Albert,' he told Dimity on his return to the rectory.

'Don't speak too soon,' his wife replied sagely.

Phil's plane was due to arrive at half-past five and Harold set off from Thrush Green soon after three o'clock.

The same quiet grey weather continued, with a raw coldness

in the air which the weather-wise said was a sure sign of snow to come.

But despite the bleak outlook, Harold was in good heart. To be driving to meet Phil again was enough to raise anyone's spirits. How would she be, he wondered? He thought of the numbed silence of the drive to the airport, with the pale girl suffering beside him.

He remembered the two ladies 'painted to the eyes' who had sat beside Phil as they drank their coffee. Out of the blue came the verse which Phil's parents must have had in mind when they chose their daughter's name.

> The ladies of St James's
> They're painted to the eyes,
> Their white it stays for ever,
> Their red it never dies:
> But Phyllida, my Phyllida!
> Her colour comes and goes;
> It trembles to a lily,—
> It wavers to a rose.

Sentimental, maybe, thought Harold as he threaded his way through the traffic, but how light and elegant! He turned the lines over in his mind, relishing their old-fashioned charm. It didn't do, he told himself, to dwell too long on 'trembling to a lily' and 'wavering to a rose'. One might as well say, 'it wobbles to a wall-flower—'.

Harold checked his straying thoughts. Whatever the merits of the poem, without doubt his favourite line was:

> But Phyllida, my Phyllida.

The years fell from him as he said it silently to himself.

The plane was punctual, and Phil smiled when her eyes lit upon him. She looked wan, and somehow smaller, than when she left, but her voice was steady when she greeted him.

He tucked a rug round her protectively when they reached the car.

'Heavens, how lovely! It's colder here than in France. My parents-in-law are flying back tomorrow and wanted me to stay on for another night, but now that all has been done – all the *awful* things – I wanted to hurry back to Jeremy.'

Harold told her that the boy had been wonderfully cheerful, but was longing to have her back.

'Do you know,' said Phil, as they neared Thrush Green, 'that when the constable told me the ghastly news, my first thought was: "I shan't have to tell Jeremy about the divorce." And then, "Thank God, I shan't have to go through all that wretched court business." It's a shameful thing, I suppose, to admit, but I felt I must tell someone, and you are just about the most understanding person to confess to.'

'It strikes me as a reasonable reaction,' replied Harold soberly. 'You've been dreading breaking the news for months now. It didn't mean that your grief was any the less. That, if I may say so, was quite evident.'

There was a long pause before the girl spoke again.

'It seems as though I've died twice. Once when he left me, and then when I heard of his death. Even now, after all this time apart, I can't imagine life without John. Whatever happens, you simply can't wipe away years of married life. The sense of loss is far, far greater than ever I imagined it would be. It's like losing an arm or a leg – some vital part. I suppose one grows numb with time, and other things happen to cover the scar, but I'm sure it will always be there.'

'Thank God I've got Jeremy, and work to do!' she added. 'Without those two things I think I should sink.'

'Never!' said Harold stoutly. 'You'll never sink. You're far too brave for that.'

They climbed the steep hill to Thrush Green. It was dark, and the lighted windows looked welcoming to the tired girl. The lights were on at Tullivers, and she looked inquiringly at Harold.

'Betty Bell and Winnie between them have made you and Jeremy a little supper, I believe. We all thought you'd prefer to be alone the first night, but if you would sooner have company, then do, please, spend the evening with me.'

Phil shook her head, smiling.

'You've thought of everything. I'll never be able to thank

you properly. I couldn't have got through this week of nightmare without you, Harold dear.'

He helped her in with her case. In the hall Jeremy and Winnie met her. After painful hugs from her son, Phil stood looking at the welcoming flowers, the fire, and the table set for two.

'Something smells delicious,' she said, sniffing the air.

'Chicken casserole,' said Winnie. 'Betty's left it all ready to serve.'

'I didn't know, until this minute, how hungry I was,' confessed Phil. 'Stop and share it, both of you.'

'No indeed,' said Winnie. 'I'm off to see to my two menfolk.'

'I'll call in the morning,' said Harold. 'Sleep well!'

Phil and Jeremy watched them depart down the path before returning to the firelit dining room.

'It's so lovely to come home,' said Phil. 'I've missed you so much.'

'Me too,' said Jeremy cheerfully, and began to tell her about the wonders of Paul Young's electric railway. The saga continued all through the meal, leaving Phil free to consider the terrible problem of when to break the news. She felt that she really could not face any more that day. It must wait until morning, she decided.

She took the boy upstairs to the bathroom and left him in the bath while she unpacked her case.

When she returned to give him a final inspection, she found him sitting very still, gazing into the distance.

'He's dead, isn't he?' he said softly.

There was no mistaking his meaning, and Phil made no pretence.

'Yes, Jeremy,' she answered. There was silence, broken only by the plopping of water dripping from a tap.

'Tell me, darling,' she said, very gently. 'How did you know?'

He looked up at her, wide-eyed and tearless.

'I saw it in your face.'

17. *Richard Contemplates Matrimony*

THE mild quiet weather continued over the Christmas season, and the inhabitants of Thrush Green were divided in their feelings towards the such unseasonably balmy weather.

The pessimists pulled long faces.

'A green Christmas means a full churchyard,' they pointed out. 'A nice sharp frost or two is what we want. Kills off the germs.'

'Kills off the old 'uns too,' retorted the warmth-lovers. 'Give us a nice mild winter – germs and all!'

The church had been lovingly decked by Winnie, Dimity, Ella and other Thrush Green ladies. Albert Piggott was still kept in bed for most of the day by Doctor Lovell, and his temper was fast deteriorating to its normal stage of moroseness. His condition was not improved by seeing fat Willie Bond, the postman, looking after St Andrew's, while he himself was laid up. There had never been any love lost between the two men since the time that Willie's vegetable marrow had beaten Albert's, by a bare inch in girth and length, at Lulling Flower Show two years earlier.

Molly was beginning to wonder how long she would have to stay with her trying old father. Ben came every weekend, but it was obvious that he was becoming impatient at the delay, and resentful of the old man's carping attitude to his poor hard-working Molly.

'It can't be helped,' Molly said, doing her best to pour oil on troubled waters. 'It won't be much longer, Ben. The minute the doctor says he can be left, I'm flying back to you and our caravan.'

And with such limited consolation Ben had to be content.

Christmas, for Phil Prior, was made less painful by the kindness of her neighbours. Jeremy's natural joy in the festivities found fulfilment at the Youngs' house, where a children's party and innumerable presents helped to put his father's tragedy into the background. The arrival of the long-awaited kitten added to his excitement. But inevitably, it was more difficult for his mother. Memories of past Christmases were inescapable.

She saw again John lighting the red candles on the Christmas tree, with wide-eyed two-year-old Jeremy gazing with wonder at each new flame. John pulling crackers, and showing Jeremy the small fireworks inside – setting fire to the 'serpent's egg', waving a minute sparkler, making a flaming paper balloon rise to the ceiling, whilst Jeremy applauded excitedly. John wrapping her in a scarlet cashmere dressing gown, which she considered madly extravagant, but adorable of him. John had always been at his best at Christmas, gay, funny, sweet, considerate. It was more than Phil could bear to think that he would never again be there to make Christmas sparkle for her.

It was strange, she thought, how the bitterness of the last year was so little remembered. The humiliation, the misery, the wretched effort of keeping things from Jeremy, were all submerged beneath the remembrances of earlier shared happiness. She marvelled at this phenomenon, but was humbly grateful that her mind worked in this way. When the subject of his father cropped up, which was not very often, Phil found that she could speak of him with true affection, keeping alive for the little boy his early memories of a loving father.

She was relieved when the New Year arrived and things returned to normal. Jeremy started school during the first week in January, and she was glad to see him engrossed in his own school affairs and friendships again. Meanwhile, she set herself to work with renewed determination.

It was plain that she must work doubly hard. John's affairs had been left tidily, with a will leaving his wife everything unconditionally. But when all had been settled, it seemed that Phil could expect a sum of only about six thousand pounds which included one or two insurances, and the sale of the furniture at the Chelsea flat. The flat itself was rented, and the firm for which he had worked had no pension schemes for dependants. There was no doubt about it – things were going to be tight if she decided to continue to live at Tullivers.

But she was determined to stay there. She loved the little house and she loved Thrush Green. The friends she had made were the dependable, kindly sort of people whose company would give her pleasure and support in the years to come, as their affection towards her, in these last few terrible weeks, had shown so clearly. She had settled in Thrush Green as snugly as a bird in its nest, and so had Jeremy. Whatever the cost, Tullivers must remain their home.

Winnie Bailey had grown particularly dear to Phil since John's death. Quiet and loving, unobtrusive, but always available, Phil found herself looking upon her as the mother she unconsciously missed. Winnie lived with anxieties herself. She knew, only too well, that her husband could not live much longer. Only constant care and rest had kept him alive so long, and the doctor himself was well aware of the fact.

'I'm living on "borrowed time", as dear old Mrs Curdle used to say,' he said matter-of-factly. 'And very lucky I am to have these few extra years.'

His complete absence of self-pity made things more bearable for Winnie, but the secret sadness was always there, and made her doubly sympathetic towards the young widow next door.

Richard, too, was unusually attentive, and made himself useful by mending a faulty lock, an electric kettle, and a pane of glass broken by Jeremy's football. He would like to have taken Phil to the theatre one evening in Oxford, but decided against it.

'The pantomime is at the New until heaven knows when,' he told his aunt impatiently, 'and the Playhouse have three weeks of something translated from the Czech, by a Frenchman, which is set in near darkness with long sessions of complete silence. I don't think Phil would find it very cheering, at the moment.'

'Take her out to lunch,' said Winnie. 'I think she'd prefer that. I know she likes to be at home when Jeremy gets back after school. He can come here for his lunch that day.'

Richard brightened.

'Kingham Mill, perhaps? "The Old Swan" at Minster Lovell? "The Shaven Crown" at Shipton-under-Wychwood?'

'Ask Phil,' advised Winnie. And so he did.

The day of their jaunt together was clear and cold. There had been a sharp frost, and the grass was still white in the shade when Phil went to the Baileys' for a drink before setting off. She found Winnie and the doctor alone, but sundry thumps overhead proclaimed that Richard was getting ready.

'He's becoming quite a Beau Brummel,' said Winnie. 'You are a good influence, Phil.'

'I don't know about that,' said her husband lightly. 'He's taking the day off for this spree.'

'Heavens!' exclaimed Phil. 'I hope I'm not taking him from his work!'

'Do him good to have a break,' said his aunt firmly.

There was a particularly heavy crash above, as though a drawer had been pulled out, too abruptly and too far, and had landed on the floor.

'It reminds me,' said the doctor ruminatively, 'of the remark made by Dr Thompson, of Cambridge, sometime in the last century. He said of Richard Jebb: "The time that Mr Jebb can spare from the adornment of his person, he devotes to the neglect of his duties." I hope that our Richard will appear as elegantly turned out as his namesake, when he *does* appear.'

He certainly looked uncommonly spruce, Phil thought, when at last he arrived, full of apologies.

'And so bad for the system, fussing and fuming,' he added. 'Otto's paper on the consequences of an overflow of adrenalin upon the digestive system is always present in my mind when I begin to get worked up. Truly horrifying, his findings were! Remind me to lend the pamphlet to you sometime.'

Ella was stumping up the path as the pair made their way to the car. They greeted each other, and Ella watched the car drive away.

'Where are they off?' asked Ella abruptly.

'They're having lunch at "The Swan",' replied Winnie. 'Come in, Ella.'

'They're not making a match of things, are they? "Going steady", as they say?'

'Really!' expostulated Winnie. 'How ridiculous you are,

Ella! Richard is simply showing a little kindness to the poor girl.'

'That's a change for Richard,' observed Ella. 'What's he hoping to get out of it?'

Winnie drew a long breath, and then let it out slowly. She had known Ella long enough to forgive her behaviour.

'What can I do for you, dear?' she asked mildly. Winnie's self-control was admirable.

The departure of the two together had been observed by several other people on Thrush Green.

Little Miss Fogerty, taking a physical education period with the infants, noticed Jeremy's mother entering the car. The children were ostensibly playing in four groups with suitable apparatus. Jeremy's group was nearest the playground railings, each child struggling to ply a skipping rope. Most of the little girls were twirling theirs adroitly enough, with expressions of smug superiority on their infant faces.

The boys, including Jeremy, were bouncing energetically but becoming hopelessly entangled with their ropes. It was whilst he was engaged in extricating himself from the loops round his ankles that Jeremy noticed his mother, and rushed to the fence to wave enthusiastically. Miss Fogerty, following his gaze, noted that Mrs Prior was accompanied – and by a bachelor!

'And so soon,' thought Miss Fogerty, sadly shocked.

'There's my mummy!' shouted Jeremy excitedly. 'And Richard! They're going to Minster Lovell. And Mrs Bailey's giving me lunch.'

'Lovely, dear,' said Miss Fogerty primly. But there was something in her tone which made Jeremy look up quickly at her little button mouth.

He resumed his clumsy skipping thoughtfully.

Harold Shoosmith was equally thoughtful. He had waved his hat cheerfully at the distant pair, as he crossed the green on his way to see Charles Henstock, but he could not ignore the involuntary spasm of concern which gripped him. Damn that fellow, Richard! He was making a confounded nuisance of himself.

As for Betty Bell, strategically placed for observation by cleaning the inside of the bedroom windows, her reactions were as straightforward as Ella's.

'*She's* not losing much time!' said Betty tartly.

The keen-eyed watchers of Thrush Green would have been singularly disappointed if they could have witnessed the innocent happenings at Minster Lovell.

The village, peaceful in its winter emptiness, showed little movement. A few wisps of blue smoke curled from the honey-coloured stone chimneys. An aged cocker spaniel, white round the muzzle, ambled vaguely along the green verge, sniffing here at a gatepost, there at a dry-stone wall.

The river Windrush purled placidly along, dimpling under the bridge, the current criss-crossed by the willow branches trailing on its surface. The ancient inn drowsed in the winter sunlight, and welcomed them with a great log fire which whispered, rather than roared. A white-haired old lady, dozing in a leather chair, scarcely stirred as they entered.

The entire village seemed to be wrapped in dreams – an atmosphere which Phil found wholly in keeping with her present state of suspended animation. Since John's death, she had gone about her daily life automatically, as though she were enclosed in an invisible shell which cut her off from everything around her. Her senses were still numbed, her reactions slow, her thoughts, when she wrote or spoke, seemed to drop from her with deadly deliberation, as slowly and stickily as cold treacle from a spoon.

If Richard could have known he would have been surprised and hurt to realize that it was this apathy which had made Phil accept his invitation in the first place. It was easier to accept than to produce an excuse when the young man had pressed her, but in truth she would have been happier getting on with a story which she had in mind.

Nevertheless, she was grateful for Richard's kindness, and believed that Winnie was glad to see them both having a brief break. She would hate to hurt Winnie, after all her concern.

The lunch was excellent, and Phil was content to let Richard do the major part of the talking. She found him interesting and remarkably astute when talking about his work, but incredibly naïve in his attitude to people.

'He's just not interested in them,' thought Phil to herself, watching him demolish caramel custard with a few swift movements. In fact, the only person he ever seemed to mention with any sort of feeling was the redoubtable Doctor Otto Goldstein. And on this subject, Richard was, without any doubt, the most crashing bore, Phil decided.

They had coffee alone by the whispering log fire, which shed a few white flakes of ash every now and again, as if to prove that the natural laws of gravity still held good even in this spell-bound lotus-land. Afterwards, they strolled up the somnolent village street towards the ruined priory. The cocker spaniel, exhausted by his morning exercise, lay sprawled on his side in the shelter of a sunny wall. He did not stir as they passed.

Walking across the shorn grass and ancient stone paths of the ruins, a wonderful sense of peace crept over Phil. Richard stopped to study a map of the site, and she walked alone into the roofless hall and gazed at the tracery of the empty windows framing the pale-blue skies of winter. A lone blackbird was perched upon one of the stone vaultings, and piped a few melancholy notes, as clear as the river water that ran nearby, and as round as the washed pebbles beneath it.

What had these venerable walls witnessed in their time, Phil wondered? Passion in plenty, bloodshed without doubt: but also piety, perseverance and simple happiness. How many people had stood here, as she did now, puzzled, unhappy, numb with pain and perplexity? And how many had found comfort in the knowledge of the continuity of life, of being but one link in a long chain of human experience, in this old, old setting?

Somehow, thought Phil, feeling the grey roughness of the ancient stones with her bare cold hand, one's own sufferings were put into perspective in the face of this survivor of the centuries. For the first time, since John had left her, a tiny tremor of hope ran through her – the faint stirring of life renewed.

T–F

They drove back slowly. Although it was barely three o'clock, the sun was low on the horizon, and the shadows of the trees lay long and straight across the bare winter fields.

'I've enjoyed it so much,' said Phil. 'It was kind of you to give me such a treat. I feel better for it.'

'I hope we can do this again,' replied Richard. 'But, of course, I shan't be at Thrush Green much longer.'

'Why, is the work nearly finished?'

'Practically. I shall have to go back to London within two or three months.'

There was a pause, while he negotiated a sharp double bend expertly, and then he spoke again.

'Would you think of coming to live in town?'

Instantly, Phil was on her guard. From his tone it was clear that the two words 'with me' might well have been added. The happy daze engendered by Minster Lovell and the sunshine fled instantly, and Phil was suddenly alert. This was a possibility of which she had not really been aware.

'I want to settle in Thrush Green,' she replied carefully. 'Both Jeremy and I are very happy there.'

'I should think you might get bored. Not many people of our age there. Besides, if you were in town you'd be on the spot for meeting your editors, wouldn't you?'

'I go up about once in three weeks to discuss things with Frank,' said Phil. 'It seems quite often enough to plan the work ahead. I'm sure I shouldn't want to call into the office more frequently, even if I were nearer.'

Richard did not reply, and Phil sensed that he was a little put out. The car's speed increased considerably, and a muscle twitched in his cheek.

Really, thought Phil, emotions of any kind were very tiresome. What was more, they were horribly exhausting. She hoped that she was wrong in imagining that Richard was interested in her – or rather, in matrimony.

She pondered on the subject as they neared Thrush Green. No doubt Richard had reached the stage when domesticity had its appeal. She suspected that anyone reasonably attractive and companionable would be eligible to Richard just now, and did not delude herself by thinking that her own personal charms had fired the young man. To be honest, would *anything* fire him?

She recalled Doctor Bailey's words. 'Richard's a cold fish,' he had said to her once. 'I'm afraid the only person Richard considers is – Richard!'

They drove up the hill from Lulling to Thrush Green. The sun had vanished behind Lulling Woods and a sharp little wind reminded the world that it was still January.

Phil sighed. It had been a lovely day, despite this small cloud between them. And whatever happened, she had Richard to thank for taking her to the tranquil ruins of Minster Lovell, and that sudden miraculous glimpse of life again after the long months following John's desertion. For that, she would always be grateful to him.

She thanked him sincerely at her gate, and he did his best to smile in return.

But there was something tight-lipped about the smile, which made it plain that Richard had been crossed, and did not like it.

Albert Piggott was one of those who saw the return of the couple. He was standing at his cottage window gazing gloomily across the green.

Willie Bond had just entered St Andrew's with a slightly pompous air of ownership which Albert found intensely irritating. What was that fat lump going to muck up now, he wondered?

He looked beyond the church to the car from which Phil emerged, his mouth curving downwards with distaste.

'Fine goings-on,' grunted Albert to Molly, who was trying to dress her fidgety son for his afternoon's outing.

'Hold still, do!' said Molly sharply. 'What goings-on, dad?'

'That young widder-woman. Setting her cap at Mrs Bailey's young fellow. Not that he's much catch, Lord alone knows, but it ain't hardly decent to go running after the men with her own poor chap scarce cold in 'is grave.'

'Maybe he's just given her a lift up from the shops,' said Molly reasonably, controlling her temper.

Albert gave a disbelieving snort.

'That's a likely tale!'

Molly buttoned George's coat with unnecessary violence.

'The trouble with you, dad, is you always thinks the worst of folks. You can't wonder you haven't got any friends.'

Albert bridled.

'Whatcher mean, no friends? What about them next door?'

'They sell beer,' said Molly roundly. 'You're a good customer. They're kind-hearted, I know, but you look around – there's not one true friend to your name!'

'That's right!' said Albert, adopting a quavering tone. 'You pitch into your poor ol' dad, just when he's too weak to stand up for hisself. I don't know what the world's comin' to when children turn on their parents. I does my best – ill though I be – to give no trouble, but you've got no proper feelings in you, you wicked hussy!'

Molly bit back the flow of words which she would willingly have poured forth, dumped George from the table to the floor, and tugged him smartly outdoors into the blessed calm of Thrush Green.

This couldn't go on, she fumed to herself, watching George stagger across to the steps which supported the statue of Nathaniel Patten, Thrush Green's famous missionary son. Jumping from the steps was the little boy's favourite activity, and Molly was glad to see him engaged so happily while she studied her problem.

When Ben had come the weekend before, Albert appeared to be rather worse, but whether this was wholly physical, or simply a way of drawing attention to himself, it was difficult to say. In any case, Molly had discussed with Ben the possibility of making their home at the cottage, in order to look after the old man.

Ben's face had clouded.

'Can't be done,' he said slowly. 'I know how you feel, but it's not right for you or George – or me, for that matter.'

He had looked across at the churchyard where his redoubt-able old grandmother lay at rest.

'And gran,' he added, 'wouldn't have let me give up her fair. And quite right too.'

'Perhaps just for the winters?' pleaded Molly, torn both ways. 'When the fair's laid up?'

'Well, I'll think about it, my love, but I don't like the idea and that's flat. You'll be nothing but a skivvy, and I'm not having that.'

Now, watching George clambering up the steps on all fours, she knew that Ben was right. She could stand it no longer. Plans would have to be made to see that the old man was provided for, and she would have a good talk with Doctor Lovell to make sure that he was not being left too soon. But go, eventually, she must.

And so, unwittingly, Phil and Richard's jaunt had brought matters to a head, in the cottage across the green, nudging into motion Albert Piggott's particular wheel of fortune.

18. *Harold Entertains an Old Friend*

ONE morning in February, Willie Marchant tacked up the hill to Thrush Green and delivered a letter to Harold Shoosmith.

Later that day Harold walked across to see Phil.

'Frank's coming down for the weekend,' he told her. 'I'm so pleased. Now I shall have a chance to repay the dozens of times I stayed at Frank's house when his wife was alive. They were so good to me when I came home on leave.'

'Bring him over for a drink,' invited Phil.

'Thank you. I know he'd love to see the cottage. But I really came to ask you and Jeremy to lunch one day, while he's here. I must get Betty Bell to whip up something rather special. He's thoroughly spoiled by Violet who housekeeps for him.'

'So Richard tells me,' said Phil.

'Richard?' exclaimed Harold. 'How does he know?'

'They belong to the same club, I gather,' said Phil, picking the kitten out of a box of new typing paper in which it was settling for a nap.

'I didn't realize they knew each other,' said Harold, looking a little put out. 'Well, well! Shall we say about twelve o'clock on Saturday?'

'That would be lovely,' agreed Phil. 'And what's more I'll give him my week's work to take back with him, and save postage.'

'That's admirably thrifty,' commented Harold with approval.

'Needs must,' laughed Phil. 'By nature I'm rather like the Flopsy Bunnies, "very improvident and cheerful," but I have to discipline myself these days.'

'How are things going, seriously?' asked Harold, emboldened by her own introduction of ways and means.

'Not too badly. I've had an introduction, through Frank, to an editor who's in charge of a number of local papers in the Midlands, and I'm starting a series of articles for him. Pretty good pay, too.'

'That's cheering news,' said Harold, rising to go. 'But don't work too hard. You ought to be having some fun now and again. What about a day out soon? Jeremy too, of course, if you'd like to bring him.'

'There's nothing I'd enjoy more,' said Phil, and meant it.

Jeremy had found a new interest since the arrival of the kitten. He had called on Dotty Harmer to report the cat's progress, and discovered the wholly delightful mode of life at the old lady's cottage.

There was no nonsense about wiping feet before entry, or having clean hands, or respectable clothing. If you arrived in the middle of one of Dotty's sketchy meals, it didn't seem to matter. As likely as not, she would be consuming a light repast as she stood at her stove or walked about the house on other affairs. As far as Jeremy could see, the meal usually consisted of a piece of brown bread, liberally spread with butter, a rough lump of cheese, and some unidentifiable leaves, by way of a salad. This seemed to be eaten at any time, followed by the crunching of a home-grown apple. Jeremy was always offered one too, and found this largesse much to his liking.

But better by far than the informality of Dotty's welcome, and the present of the apple, was the large number of animals which made up Dotty's family. The goats in particular, fascinated the boy and he even drank the milk whilst it was still warm from the animal, with uncommon relish, which Dotty heartily approved.

One spring Saturday morning he bounded down the path by Albert Piggott's cottage and gained the path leading to Dotty's and finally to Lulling Woods. The air was balmy, his spirits high, and he carried a large bunch of grass and greenery from the hedges as a present for Daisy, the milker, and Dulcie, the younger goat.

Charles Henstock privately thought that Dulcie was poorly named – neither sweet nor gentle, and very quick to use her horns on unsuspecting visitors, as he had found to his cost one wet day. His clerical grey trousers had never completely recovered from their immersion in the puddle in which Dulcie's sly butting had landed him. Jeremy, however, was rather more alert to Dulcie's wiles, and his passion for her was unclouded.

On this particular morning he found Dotty in a somewhat agitated mood. She was having difficulty in fixing a chain to Dulcie's collar. Daisy, taking advantage of the disturbance, was adding gleefully to the chaos by bleating continuously, and rushing round and round in circles so that her tethering chain was soon shortened to a couple of feet. This gave her the opportunity to bleat even more madly, puffing noisily between bleats to prove how sorely she was being tried.

Dulcie, unduly skittish, kicked up her heels every time that Dotty approached her. Dotty, red in the face, greeted Jeremy shortly.

'Get Daisy undone, boy, will you? And give her some of that stuff you've brought to stop her row.'

Jeremy obediently accomplished this task. In the comparative peace that followed, Dotty captured the younger goat, and sighed noisily with relief.

'Where's Dulcie going?' asked Jeremy.

'To be mated,' said Dotty flatly.

'What d'you mean – *mated*?' queried Jeremy.

'Married, then,' said Dotty, hitching up a stocking in a preoccupied way.

'*Married*? But only *people* get married,' exclaimed Jeremy.

'I know that,' said Dotty, nettled. Dulcie began to tug powerfully at her lead.

'But you said—'

'Here, you clear off home,' said Dotty forthrightly. 'I'm up to my eyes this morning, as you can see.'

The boy retreated very slowly backwards.

'Will she have baby goats when she's been mated?'

'*Kids*, you mean,' said Dotty pedantically. 'Do use the right expressions, child.'

'Well, will she?'

'What?' said Dotty, stalling for time.

'Have baby goats. Kids, I mean?'

'Maybe,' said Dotty, with unusual caution. Difficult to know how much children knew about the facts of life these days, and anyway it wasn't her business to enlighten this one.

'Can I have one when they come, Miss Harmer?' begged Jeremy longingly. '*Please*, can I?'

Dotty's slender stock of patience suddenly ran out at her heels like gunpowder. Her voice roared out like a cannon.

'Look, boy! I don't know *if* she'll have kids, *when* she'll have kids, or if your mother would let you have one if she *did* have kids! You're far too inquisitive, and a confounded nuisance. Get off home!'

She raised a skinny, but powerful, arm, and Dulcie, sensing joyous combat, lowered her head for action. In the face of this combined attack, Jeremy fled, but even as he ran determined to come again as soon as things at Dotty's had returned once more to their usual chaotic normality.

Meanwhile, he decided, slackening his pace as the distance between Dotty's and his own breathless form increased, he must set about persuading his mother that a little kid would be very useful for keeping Tullivers' grass down. But, somehow, he sensed that that would be an uphill battle.

Frank arrived the following weekend, in the midst of a torrential rainstorm. Ella Bembridge, struggling to shut an upstairs window to keep out the deluge, was the first to see the beautiful sleek Jaguar creep through Harold's gateway. She knew whose it must be, for Dimity had told her all about Harold's friend, his redoubtable Violet, and the fact that he was a busy editor. If Frank had been aware how much was known about him already at Thrush Green he would have been very surprised.

'What a welcome for you!' exclaimed Harold, opening the front door. 'Come in, my dear fellow, before you are wet through.'

He showed his friend to his bedroom and went downstairs again to prepare drinks. From the kitchen, delicious smells of lunch emanated.

'Not quite up to Violet's standards, I'm afraid,' said Harold, when his friend reappeared, 'but pretty good, nevertheless. By the way, Mrs Prior and her boy are joining us for lunch.'

'How nice!' said Frank. 'Whereabouts is her house?'

Harold pointed out Tullivers through the veils of slashing rain.

'If this doesn't stop, I must fetch her,' said Harold. 'It will save her getting out her car. She could get soaked just going to her garage.'

It occurred to Frank that Harold was rather unduly solicitous.

'Mine's out already,' he said. 'We'll fetch her together.'

But, as it happened, the storm swept away before Phil and Jeremy needed to set out, and by the time they arrived, the sun was turning the puddles on Thrush Green to dazzling mirrors.

Betty Bell, who had heard quite enough of the paragon Violet to be put on her mettle, brough forth a superb steak and kidney pudding swathed in a snowy napkin. The Brussels sprouts, the braised celery and the floury potatoes were all at the peak of perfection, and a truly enormous orange trifle, decorated with almonds and crystallized orange segments made Jeremy sigh with ecstasy.

'And if that Violet can do better than that,' said Betty grimly to herself as she returned to the kitchen, 'I'll eat my hat!'

After lunch, the three friends sat and talked over coffee, while Jeremy lay on the floor with volumes of *Punch* around him. It was a happy relaxed little party, mellowed by Betty's superb cooking and Harold's good wine, but Frank was alert enough to notice the attentions which his old friend Harold gave to the young woman, and thought that they were perhaps a trifle warmer than ordinary civility dictated. Could this confirmed bachelor, now approaching sixty, have designs on his promising new contributor?

It looked highly probable, thought Frank, sipping his coffee, but who would have suspected it?

Just before three, Phil and Jeremy departed.

'We'll look forward to seeing you both tomorrow about half-past six,' said Phil. 'I've asked the Baileys to come in to meet you. And Richard.'

When they had gone, the two friends settled by the fire again.

'An attractive girl,' said Frank cautiously, 'and very sound as a writer. I have you to thank for introducing her to me, Harold.'

'We're all very fond of her here,' replied Harold. 'I can't make up my mind if her husband's sudden death was a good thing or not. She was dreading the court proceedings, and telling the boy, of course. A messy business – but she was terribly shocked by his death. I wonder if she'll ever get over it.'

'Be married in six months,' said Frank robustly, producing a pipe and ramming home a generous pinch of tobacco. 'Got any eligible young men nearby?'

A faint look of distaste crept over Harold's face, and was observed by the wily Frank.

'There's Richard. You know him, I believe?'

'Slightly. I see him at the club, but he's such a crashing bore about his insides I give him a wide berth, I don't mind admitting.'

'Phil seems to like him, nevertheless.'

'Does she?' said Frank thoughtfully.

They leant back in their armchairs, pondering on the idiosyncrasies of women.

'I shouldn't think he stands a chance,' said Frank, at length. 'She's too much sense to take on a fellow like that. Why, he thinks of no one but himself!'

Harold brightened a little.

'That's how I feel. How I *hope*, perhaps I should say. But then, after all, they are much of an age, and she might think that marriage would improve Richard.'

'Any woman who marries a man expecting to improve him,' said Frank tartly, 'deserves all she gets – and that's disappointment. No, Phil won't be so foolish, I feel positive.'

He tapped his pipe briskly on the bars of the grate.

'But you say you *hope* she won't marry Richard, Harold,' he went on. 'Perhaps I shouldn't ask, but tell me, are you at all interested?'

There was a little silence before Harold replied. Outside, the rooks cawed above the chestnut avenue, and the sound of distant church bells told of a Saturday afternoon wedding.

'Yes, I am,' said Harold very quietly, looking down at his clasped hands. 'But to be truthful, I find it hard to sort out my feelings. I love my present way of life. I'm not at all sure that marriage would suit me, and in any case, I can't see that it would be fair to ask a young woman like that to take on a man of my age.'

'You're only five years my senior,' pointed out Frank. 'I still look upon myself as a spry young-middle-ager.'

'You've always been young for your years, anyway,' answered Harold. 'I've knocked about such a lot, I sometimes feel older than mine.'

'Try your luck,' said Frank spontaneously.

'Too early yet,' replied Harold. 'Let her get over her tragedy first, I think. Besides, do I really want to get married? That's the test, I think. Surely I should be more whole-hearted about this affair? What do you think, Frank? You know I value your opinions.'

Frank took a long pull at his pipe.

'I hate to give any advice in a case like this. But I do just wonder, Harold, if your kind heart and old-fashioned sense of chivalry are rather pushing you into this offer of marriage. To my mind, you are a perfectly-balanced person on your own – self-sufficient without being self-satisfied, a truly rare combination. You may well find that matrimony complicates your well-ordered existence, and puts more of a strain on you than you had imagined. On the other hand, as I know full well, marriage can make a man. I miss Margaret more than I can say.'

'That I can understand. She was a fine woman in every way. But not having been so blessed, I've no experience. No, Frank, reason tells me that it would not be fair to Phil – she'd probably spend the last few years of my life as a nurse – appalling thought! And I don't think I really want to give up my selfish way of life.'

'Put the whole affair out of your mind for a month or two,' said Frank. 'You'll both know your feelings better by then.'

'Good old Time,' agreed Harold quietly. 'I'm sure you're right.'

He got up and fetched a map from his desk, closing the subject of Phil Prior.

'I thought we'd drive out to Lechlade for a meal tonight,' he said. 'Which way shall we go?'

The two friends held the map between them and plans for the distant future were forgotten in making those for the evening.

The tiny sitting room at Tullivers just held the six grown-ups comfortably, and Jeremy, as the important seventh, made himself useful in passing salted nuts and other delicious morsels to his seniors whilst managing to dispatch a generous selection on his own account.

Frank found Doctor Bailey a fascinating companion. They were both fishing enthusiasts, and the doctor regaled the younger man with tales of past exploits on the Windrush.

'You must come down again and try your luck on the Lechlade stretch,' said the doctor. 'I've several old friends there who would be delighted to give you a day's sport.'

He nodded across the room to Richard.

'Our nephew there,' he continued, 'isn't interested, more's the pity.'

Richard was making himself particularly charming to Phil. Since their outing, she had taken care not to meet him alone, but was glad of this opportunity to repay his invitation in the company of others.

There was no doubt about it, thought Frank privately, Richard showed up to greater advantage here than in town. And he was a personable young man, and certainly going to be a very successful one. Harold seemed to have a rival here.

He watched his hostess's reaction to Richard's attentions, but could perceive nothing more than ordinary politeness on her part.

The cottage he found charming, and delighted Phil by saying so when she showed him round.

'It's the perfect place to work,' she told him. 'Small enough to keep tidy easily, and gives me a peaceful base when Jeremy's at school.'

'I think I've got an American magazine interested in a

longish short story from you, sometime in the future. Perhaps a Christmas story? Like the idea?'

'*Rather!*' cried Phil warmly.

'I'll tell you more when you come up next week,' promised Frank.

That evening he said farewell to his old friend Harold, being careful not to mention the confidences which he had been given earlier.

'Come to me for a weekend in April,' were his last words before setting off, and Harold promised that he would.

Frank drove home speedily, his thoughts full of Thrush Green and its inhabitants.

What did the future hold for them, he wondered?

19. *Richard Tries His Luck*

SPRING seemed a long time in coming to Thrush Green, and people were getting heartily sick of being housebound.

Keen gardeners, such as Harold, fretted at the delay in planting early potatoes and vegetable seeds. The lawns were as tousled and rough as unshaven old men, and the mowers, oiled and waiting to be used, had to wait still longer as snow showers and cold rain kept the ground soggy.

Molly's father developed a mild attack of bronchitis which meant that her departure must be delayed.

'Done it a-purpose, I shouldn't wonder,' commented Ben, who was chafing at Molly's enforced absence from her own home.

'Just till he's over this,' Molly pleaded. 'I must stay till he's back on his feet, Ben. I don't relish it, you know that, but who's to do for him?'

At the school, Miss Watson and Miss Fogerty looked forward to the end of term. Measles and mumps had taken their toll in February and March, and the bitter weather had meant that play outside was impossible. Tempers became frayed, and the fact that the school was most sketchily cleaned did not help matters.

Mrs Cooke of Nidden, who had come back temporarily 'to oblige', was no Nelly Piggott when it came to elbow grease, and Miss Watson and Miss Fogerty were often to be seen sweeping up the classrooms which, in theory, had already been done by Mrs Cooke.

'But what else can we do?' asked Miss Watson despairingly of Miss Fogerty, two days before term ended. 'I had a word with Molly Curdle. She'd be perfect, of course, living so near and being such a good worker, but she's too tied with George and that dreadful old father to consider it. In any case, it would only be a temporary arrangement again.'

Matters came to a head when Mrs Cooke arrived on the last

day of term. She wore a look of smug importance, as she carried her broom into Miss Watson's room. The children had departed, excited at the thought of three weeks' holiday, and bearing home their term's drawings to show their resigned mothers. As most of these were executed in chalk, and were being clutched face down against winter coats, their reception at home might be expected to be bleak indeed.

'I thought I'd tell you straight off,' said Mrs Cooke cheerfully, 'that I'm not to do any more work. Doctor's orders.'

'Good heavens!' exclaimed Miss Watson. 'What's the matter?'

'Another little stranger on the way,' replied Mrs Cooke, with immense satisfaction.

Miss Watson's mind was in confusion. Could Mrs Cooke's pleasure really come from the thought of yet another addition to her large, dirty and unruly family? Or was she simply pleased to have a good excuse to leave the school in the lurch? Miss Watson, a realist, was inclined to think that the latter reason caused Mrs Cooke's evident smugness.

'Will you be able to cope with the holiday scrubbing?' asked Miss Watson, knowing the answer before the question was finished.

'Not a hope,' replied Mrs Cooke triumphantly. 'I'm inclined to miscarry if I does too much. It's a weak sort of uterus, you might say. Doctor said something about a prolapse. You know what that is?' asked Mrs Cooke darkly.

'No, I don't,' replied Miss Watson shortly. What a blessing to be a spinster, was her heartfelt thought!

'Well, that's that, I suppose, Mrs Cooke,' she continued resignedly. 'I must thank you for stepping into the breach. You'll sweep up now, will you?'

'I'll oblige,' said Mrs Cooke, inclining her head regally, and set about her limited labours.

'Would you have thought it?' asked Miss Watson of Miss Fogerty later. 'I gather she's still feeding that last baby – Adrian, or Clifford, or whatever it is. Frankly, I lose count of them.'

'It's a common fallacy,' pronounced Miss Fogerty importantly, 'that a woman who is feeding a child cannot fall again.'

Miss Watson looked at her assistant in astonishment.

'Agnes, dear,' she protested, 'how on earth do you know such things?'

'I always read the mothers' page under the dryer at the hairdresser's,' answered little Miss Fogerty imperturbably.

She skewered her good velour hat to her skimpy bun, and the two ladies made their way outside.

'But this doesn't solve our problem, does it?' said Miss Fogerty, pausing in the chilly porch.

Next door, Harold Shoosmith's gate clanged as Betty Bell set off home on her bicycle. Rosy and bright-eyed, as fresh as when she had arrived at work some hours earlier, she waved energetically to the two ladies in the school porch, before pedalling away briskly down the hill.

Miss Watson looked at Miss Fogerty, rather as stout Cortez looked upon the peaks of Darien, so long ago.

'Dare we?' she whispered.

'Why not!' said little Miss Fogerty robustly.

It was in April that Richard's work at Oxford came to an end, and as the time approached, Winnie Bailey was mightily relieved.

In all fairness, she admitted, that although Richard had stayed longer than was at first intended, he had really been very little trouble, and had more than pulled his weight by tackling little jobs about the house which were beyond her own understanding and the doctor's strength.

Nevertheless, the thought of having the house to themselves again was heart-lifting. She wondered, sometimes, about the relationship between her nephew and the young widow next door. She had noticed that the outing *à deux* had not been repeated, and that since that day Richard had been unduly restless, but nothing had been said, and in any case, Winnie would not have expected to hear about such a personal matter from Richard.

It was all the more surprising, therefore, when he broached the subject one Sunday morning at breakfast time. The doctor was still in bed, having had a restless night, and Winnie and her nephew lingered over their coffee.

Richard was busy grating a raw apple into a bowl of rolled oats, pine kernels, sultanas and milk – a mixture which he concocted each morning for himself from a recipe of Otto's.

It was a messy business, and Winnie watched the operation resignedly.

'Why don't you eat the apple separately?' she asked.

Richard looked up from his work in some surprise.

'My dear aunt, that would quite defeat Otto's object. The enzymes in the saliva react in a truly magical way upon the mixture of minerals in this bowl. Wonderfully purging, and marvellously toning to the lining of the digestive tract. A friend of Otto's claims to have cured dyspeptic ulcers with this mixture alone.'

He continued to grate energetically, stirred up the mash, and ate it with much relish.

Winnie watched him as she sipped her coffee.

'I've been meaning to tell you about my immediate plans, Aunt Win,' he said, when at last the bowl was empty. 'I really do appreciate your hospitality. You've both been so kind. I hope I haven't been too much of a nuisance.'

Winnie reassured him on this point.

'Well now, I ought to be off in a week or two's time. The point is that the Carslakes have offered me their house while he has a year at Harvard as a visiting professor. They're asking only a nominal rent – they really want someone to keep an eye on things, I gather, and of course it would suit me perfectly.'

'And you are going to accept?'

'It all depends.'

'What on? It seems straightforward enough to me.'

For once in his life Richard appeared discomfited. The vestiges of a blush were apparent to Winnie's sharp eyes.

'The point is,' said Richard, pushing back his chair and walking to the window, 'I've been thinking of getting married, and I suppose the girl would like to see the house first. Hardly fair to take her there if she loathed the place.'

'Quite so,' agreed Winnie. 'And who have you in mind?'

'Why, Phil Prior!' exclaimed Richard. 'Surely you realized that I was interested?'

'I knew you liked her,' said Winnie guardedly, 'but not that you hoped to marry her.'

'Aunt Winnie,' said Richard, returning to the table and looking down at his aunt pleadingly. 'Do you think I've a chance? Has she said anything to you about me?'

'Nothing at all,' confessed Winnie, 'except to say how beautifully you'd cleaned out the drain.'

'Hardly a sufficient basis for marriage!' observed Richard, with a wry smile. 'But I suppose I can count it as half a point in my favour.'

He wandered back to the window, hands in his pockets. Something about the slouched back, the ruffled fair hair and general air of desolation, touched Winnie's kind heart.

'You could always ask her,' she pointed out.

'But what hopes, d'you think?'

'Who knows?' said Winnie. 'But why not try your luck?'

She began to pile the coffee cups on to the tray. Richard continued to stand, glooming out upon the garden with unseeing eyes. She wondered what effect this preoccupation with love would have upon Richard's fickle digestion.

He was certainly not her idea of a husband, thought Winnie, bearing the tray towards the kitchen.

Nor, she thought with some satisfaction, Phil Prior's, if she knew anything about that sensible young woman.

'Here,' cried Betty Bell to her employer one morning. 'Got something to tell you! I've got a new job!'

'Betty!' exclaimed Harold, dumbfounded. As everyone knows, one of the most heinous crimes which can be committed in a small community is inveigling someone else's domestic worker into coming to work for oneself. Many a deep friendship has been wrecked by such perfidy, and Harold could not believe that Betty Bell would be a party to such treachery.

'You're not going to leave me?' pleaded the stricken man.

Betty's hearty peal of laughter set the silver ringing on the sideboard.

'Now, would I do a thing like that? No, I was just pulling your leg. Made you sit up though, didn't it, eh?'

'It certainly did. But, tell me, what's all this about?'

Betty settled herself comfortably on the edge of the dining room table. Harold, forewarned, shifted the remains of his breakfast out of harm's way.

'Well, it's like this. Mrs Cooke's expecting again – '

'No!' broke in Harold.

'Strue! Like rabbits, ain't it? Well, as I was saying, she's off work for a bit – if she was ever *on*, if you take my meaning – and them two poor old things next door are up to their hocks in dirt in that school, so they've asked me if I'd help 'em out.'

'Oh,' said Harold, 'and what have you replied?'

Betty suddenly became rather distant and adopted the air of one-who-knew-her-place.

'I said I must ask your permission, sir. They was going to come and have a word with you themselves, but I said let me sound you out. If you was going to be funny about it, I said I'd turn the job down.'

'What does it mean – from my point of view?' asked Harold cautiously.

'If you was willing, I'd come to you half an hour earlier, as soon as I'd done in there in the morning.'

'Humph!' said Harold, considering the matter. It seemed reasonable enough, and he knew Betty could do with the extra money which the school job would provide.

'Very well,' he agreed. 'Let's see how it works out.'

'You're a real gentleman!' cried Betty, bouncing off the table energetically. Harold retrieved a spoon which had been whisked to the floor by her skirt. 'I'll call in next door on my way home and tell the poor old soul!'

'I'll call on Miss Watson myself,' said Harold. 'I'm glad to be of some help to the lady.'

'You'll be mentioned in her prayers tonight,' said Betty heartily. 'And to tell you the truth, in mine too, Mr Shoosmith.

Money's not easy to come by these days, and I'm thankful to get a bit of extra work.'

She whirled from the room and very soon Harold heard her voice raised in song as she polished the bathroom floor.

Harold smiled to himself. She really was a wonderful girl. He supposed he must be prepared to share his good luck with Thrush Green School. If Betty Bell took on the job, she would certainly do it splendidly.

It was, in fact, the school's luckiest day, for Betty Bell was to keep it spotless and shining for many a long year.

Two days after Richard's breakfast conversation with his aunt, the young man dressed himself with some care and made his way next door.

Dusk was falling, and although the weather still remained cold, a few early daffodils had braved the April winds, and the sticky buds in the avenue of chestnut trees were beginning to break into leaf.

The birds were busy struggling with wisps of dry grass, feathers, and other nesting material. It seemed a propitious time for a young man to go a-wooing, and Richard approached the late admiral's dolphin knocker in the appropriately nervous condition brought on by mingled hope and ardour.

Phil answered the door with a bath towel thrown over one shoulder, her hair in a state of disarray and a blue streak across one cheek, which had been made, Richard guessed correctly, by a ball-point pen, and would, he had no doubt, be the very devil to remove.

'Do come in,' she said somewhat distractedly. 'I'm just giving Jeremy a quick once-over before he puts on his pyjamas. He's rather like a cat in his ablutions – terribly busy working on one or two square inches, and completely neglecting the rest.'

She led the way to the sitting-room and handed him a decanter and a glass.

'Help yourself, Richard. I'll be back in a tick.'

Richard poured himself an inch of dry sherry. Otto did not approve of alcohol, but Richard felt that on this occasion even the stern Otto would have relaxed his rules. And as he had once said to his disciple, 'If you *must* drink such liver-rotting poison as sherry, then drink the dryest you can find.'

He sat there twirling his little glass disconsolately. Having girded himself for the endeavour, it was doubly hard to have the event postponed, even for a few minutes. He realized that he must approach the delicate proposal with some preliminaries, but he had decided that they must be as short as ordinary civility demanded. He was no speech-maker, and he had wisely made no rehearsals. He felt it best to rely on the spontaneous promptings of his feelings.

When Phil returned, she had combed her hair, miraculously removed the blue streak, and generally looked her usual neat and attractive self.

'May I pour you one?' asked Richard.

'Thanks. I can do with it. I always think that the time between tea-time and bed-time is the most exhausting for mothers. Just when one is most tired is the time when most is demanded.'

She accepted the sherry gratefully, put her feet up on a footstool, and sighed happily.

'But what brings you here, Richard? I hear from Winnie you are leaving us very soon. Will you be sorry?'

Such an abrupt approach to the matter in hand took Richard off his guard. He swallowed awkwardly, and set himself spluttering, as a drop of sherry went down the wrong way.

'Let me get you some water,' said Phil, getting to her feet, and viewing her scarlet-faced visitor with concern.

'All right now,' he gasped huskily, still fighting for breath. What a way to go about a proposal of marriage, thought Richard!

Phil resumed her seat.

'I always think it's extraordinary,' she remarked, 'how violently the body reacts to something in the windpipe.'

'Good thing it does,' responded Richard. 'You'd soon croak if it didn't!'

An amicable silence fell. A tiny jet of flame hissed from a crack in the coal in the fireplace. The clock ticked companionably above it, and outside the birds shrilled and piped before going to roost for the night.

Richard, now recovered, felt that he must return to the subject of his departure. He put down his glass carefully.

'You asked if I should miss Thrush Green, and I certainly shall. Uncle Donald and Aunt Winnie have been very patient, and so good to me.'

'They're absolute darlings,' agreed Phil warmly. 'Don't you agree?'

Richard refused to be side-tracked.

'But the person I shall miss most of all,' said Richard firmly, 'will be you.'

'Me?' cried Phil, with mingled surprise and dismay. 'But we've had very little to do with each other, after all.'

'I should like to think,' said Richard, warming to his theme, 'that we could be a great deal together in the future.'

'How do you mean?' asked Phil, her heart sinking. She rose and poured herself another glass of sherry. If this were to be a proposal of marriage, she could do with a little support, she told herself.

Richard launched into a long explanation of the Carslakes' offer of their house for a year, and before he was halfway through the saga, Phil could foresee the outcome.

'And there is no one in the world,' declared Richard, with more warmth in his voice than Phil had ever heard before, 'I should like to share it with, more than you yourself. It may seem a roundabout way of asking you to consider marrying me, but if you could – ?'

His voice faltered to a halt, and his blue eyes were full of pleading. At that moment, Phil found him more alive, more attractive, more lovable than she would ever have thought possible. It was a pity that his Uncle Donald could not see the 'cold fish' now. For this one fleeting moment, Richard was a warm human being. Rare emotion had shaken him into life at long last.

'Could you?' he asked earnestly.

'Oh, Richard!' exclaimed Phil, genuinely moved. 'I hate to upset you – I really do. But it would never work, you know.

We're not in the least – what's the word I want – *compatible*.'

'We could try,' said Richard.

Phil shook her head.

'No, we couldn't,' she said gently. Already, the mutinous little-boy-crossed look had come into Richard's face. 'In some ways, I'm so much older than you are. I'm a lot further along the road of experience, for one thing, with a marriage behind me and a boy to bring up. And then, in so many ways, you are much cleverer than I am. I'm afraid you would soon be impatient of my shortcomings. I know nothing of your work. You know nothing of mine. There's so little to hold us together, Richard.'

Richard's gaze was downcast. The hissing coal fell from the fire and smouldered, unheeded, on the hearth. Somewhere, on the other side of Thrush Green, a child called to another, and a man went by Tullivers, tapping rhythmically with his walking stick.

These little outside noises seemed to break the spell of silence.

'Well, that's that, I suppose,' said Richard mournfully. 'I'm disappointed, but I'm not surprised. I suppose I'm not what Aunt Winnie would call "much catch". I've never had anyone to consider but myself. It makes a man selfish, but if you had felt you could marry me, I think it would have been the making of me.'

And what about me? was Phil's silent rejoinder. She surveyed the young man for a few moments, wondering if she should speak her mind or not.

She made her decision. She had nothing to lose. Richard, and perhaps another girl one day in the future, had much to gain.

'Richard, of course I'm grateful for being asked to think of marrying you, but do you realize that not once have you said you want me to marry you because you love me? I'm not a romantic woman, heaven knows, but you'll meet a great many who are, and *any* woman will want to be assured that she is loved before she enters marriage. Who on earth is going to get married without it?'

'But you must know that I shouldn't have asked you if I didn't love you!' protested Richard.

'Then say so,' said Phil, with some asperity. 'I think you will marry eventually – probably very soon, but you'll have to put your under-worked heart, as well as your over-worked head, into persuading any normal girl to take you on.'

She paused, and Richard rose to depart. Had she gone too far?

'I'm sorry to hurt you,' she said impulsively, 'but someone must tell you. No hard feelings?'

'Of course not,' said Richard. 'I'll think over what you've said.'

He held out a hand.

'I probably shan't see you again. I'll move into Carslake's place as soon as I can.'

Phil ignored the hand, and kissed him gently on the cheek.

'Dear Richard! Don't take it too badly, and look out for someone who really will make you a good wife one day. Thank you for being so kind, always, to me and Jeremy.'

Richard's blue eyes blinked rapidly as he turned away.

Phil accompanied him to the front door. The green was dark now, and the light at the corner by the pillar box silhouetted the writhing branches of the chestnut trees.

At the gate he turned and raised his hand to his fair hair in the semblance of a salute.

It was to be a very long time before Phil Prior ever saw Richard again.

20. *An Engagement*

It was May before Molly managed to rejoin Ben. The fair had come as usual to Thrush Green on the first day of that month, but, as the doctor said to Winnie, it wasn't the same without Mrs Curdle to run it.

'And I still expect a bouquet of artificial flowers,' confessed Winnie. 'Embarrassingly large though it was, and really quite hideous, I loved her for bringing it.'

All the children of Thrush Green had spent a hilarious few hours on the simple swings and roundabouts, the coconut shies and side-stalls of Ben Curdle's little fair. Jeremy and Paul had tried everything, and Jeremy had presented his mother with a hard-won vase of shocking pink with heavy gilding, and a very small goldfish in a jam jar. These treasures she had accepted with praiseworthy, if mendacious, expressions of delight.

When the fair closed down that night, after its one-day stand, Ben and Molly sat in Albert's kitchen and talked of their plans. Upstairs, Albert snored noisily. In the next bedroom young George, thumb in mouth, slept just as soundly.

'Doctor Lovell says he can manage pretty well on his own, and I've made arrangements for him to have a hot dinner at "The Two Pheasants" next door every day,' said Molly. 'At least for a bit.'

'And who pays for that?' asked Ben.

Molly looked confused.

'Couldn't we do that, Ben? You know how he's placed and – '

Ben cut her short with a hug.

'Anything to get you back,' he told her cheerfully. 'I'll go round and settle things with them. But knowing your dad, I reckon it would be best to do this a month at a time. See how things go with him. If he gets hitched up again, he won't need it!'

'I can't see anyone being fool enough to take him on,' admitted Molly. 'He's nigh on killed me this last few months.'

And so it was arranged. A week later Molly was ready to go. The cottage was spruce, the larder well stocked, with a fruit cake in the cake tin, and a steak and kidney pie in the larder. Her father's linen was washed, ironed and mended, and Molly said goodbye to him thankfully. She set out with little George on her lap and with Ben at the wheel, to go back to her own life.

They drove slowly across the green, Molly waving to the bent figure of Albert standing pathetically in the cottage doorway. Thrush Green had its newly-washed, innocent, early morning look – the wide grassy spaces bare of figures, the rooks circling lazily above the church.

Molly felt a pang at leaving it all. There was nowhere as dear as Thrush Green, and despite her father's niggardly ways, she felt a certain sympathy with the old man.

Ben, knowing her gentle heart, put a comforting hand on her knee as the car slid down the hill to Lulling.

'He'll do,' said Ben, and added wickedly, 'the devil looks after his own.'

Later that day, the rector found Albert Piggott walking briskly around the churchyard. He carried no walking stick, and although he was thinner and paler than usual, he seemed remarkably spry. He was inspecting old Mrs Curdle's grave. Ben had decked it with tulips and daffodils. At every visit he had thus honoured the memory of his much-loved grandmother, and even Albert's flinty heart was touched.

'Why, Albert,' cried the rector, with genuine joy, 'how well you look! I'd no idea you were getting on so famously!'

Albert acknowledged the kindness with a perfunctory nod.

'Got to do for meself now, sir, so I'd best get used to it. I was thinking I might manage the church again if you're so minded.'

'But, of course!' exclaimed the rector, delighted. 'If you are sure you feel up to it.'

Albert's face took on its usual woebegone and cautious look.

'I don't say as I could do the graves. I'm past that sort of work – but the boiler, now, and any little inside jobs as I used to do, well – I reckons I can struggle along with they.'

'I'm sure we can come to some arrangement with Willie about the heavy work,' Charles Henstock assured him. 'Now look after yourself, Albert, and don't stay out too long in this treacherous wind.'

He returned to the rectory in high spirits.

'Dimity, my dear,' he declared to his wife, 'Albert Piggott's made a truly remarkable return to health. He was actually walking without a stick! Think of that!'

'I am,' said Dimity drily. 'Now that Molly's gone he can finish with his acting.'

The rector made his way thoughtfully to his study. As a student of human nature, he gave his keen-eyed wife full marks. But who would have thought it?

Sometime later that month, Ella Bembridge strode across the green to collect her goat's milk from Dotty.

At last the weather had relented. May, the loveliest of months, was warm and sunny, and as if to make up for lost time, the leaves and flowers burst out of their sheaths and filled the air with glory.

Butterflies and tortoises emerged from their long hibernation. Bees hummed among the wallflowers, and the cats of Thrush Green sunned themselves on the warm stone walls.

Ella found Dotty watching the antics of Dulcie's new twin kids. They were a skewbald pair, white and brown, and already as nimble and wicked as their proud mother. They skittered away, prancing sideways, their eyes upon Ella as she approached.

'A handsome pair,' commented Ella, wisely keeping her distance from Dulcie. She knew, from painful experience, that Dulcie had a way of running rapidly round a person's legs, trapping them in her chain, and bringing them heavily to the ground. It was a pastime which never palled for Dulcie. The unwilling victims failed to see the joke.

'Got homes for them?' asked Ella.

'I shall keep one,' said Dotty, 'and that Prior child wants one; but whether his mother does, I don't know.'

'Not much room at Tullivers,' observed Ella.

'Well, I suppose she may well be at Harold Shoosmith's before the year's out,' said Dotty reasonably. 'Now Winnie's Richard has left the coast clear, I can't think why Harold doesn't move in for the kill.'

Ella, forthright as she was, could not help feeling that Dotty's expressions were rather stronger than necessary.

'Maybe he doesn't want to get married. And anyway, they may prefer to live at Tullivers, if they do make a match of it.'

'Doubtful,' said Dotty, taking out a man's red and white spotted handkerchief from her skirt pocket, and blowing her nose with a resounding trumpeting. 'Too pokey for Harold. All those cups and things he's got. And he's used to large rooms, living out in Africa, with all those natives fanning him.'

'Got any goat's milk?' asked Ella abruptly. The conversation seemed to be getting out of hand, and Dotty, once started, was deucedly difficult to stop.

'Well, for the kid's sake, I hope they make up their minds quickly,' continued Dotty, leading the way through a rabble of hopeful hens to the house, 'and plump for Harold's place. Plenty of good grass there, and a nice hazel hedge. I shall rely on you, Ella, to do your best to further this affair.'

'Who do you think I am?' cried Ella. 'Dan Cupid? If you ask me, Harold Shoosmith's quite capable of doing his own work. He knows his own mind, mark my words!'

But, if the truth were known, Harold was only now coming to know his own mind.

He had been at Frank's when Richard departed, and learnt from the Baileys about the young man's haste to go, after his visit to Tullivers.

'Sent him away with a flea in his ear,' said the old doctor, with some relish. 'Can't blame her, can you?'

'I think you're misjudging her,' said Winnie. 'She's too kind to deal over-ruthlessly with Richard. But you know how he is – hates to be crossed. He's been hopelessly spoilt ever since he was a child. He was bound to take this badly.'

'How is she?' asked Harold.

'As cheerful as ever. Very busy writing for your friend, as you know. She's said nothing to me about Richard's proposal. Probably thinks I don't know, but he burst in here that night, looking as black as thunder, and simply said: "She won't have me. I'm off next week!" And that was it.'

It certainly brought matters to a head for Harold, and as the days slipped by he studied his feelings as dispassionately as he could. There was no doubt about it. The girl was very dear to him, but the longer he postponed his decision to speak, the more certain he became that marriage was not for him.

All the arguments that he and Frank had discussed, when his friend visited Thrush Green, were gone over again. When Harold had stayed with Frank, only a week or so before, little had been said on the matter, except that Harold had intimated that he felt that he could not expect an attractive young woman like Phil to take him on, and that his own feelings were, perhaps, as Frank had once suggested, a compound of pity and protectiveness.

The more he thought about it, the stronger grew his conviction that he would never be accepted, even if he were brave enough to ask her. Time, his old ally, seemed to be slow in coming to his aid, and he was still troubled in his mind when he called at Tullivers, one fine morning at the end of May, to help Phil in her kitchen garden.

Their combined efforts had made it one of the tidiest and most attractive gardens at Thrush Green. Harold surveyed, with pleasure, the double row of sturdy broad beans, and the neat labels which showed where carrots, early potatoes and beetroot had been planted. The currant and gooseberry bushes, which he had rescued from suffocation last autumn, were making vigorous growth, and Phil's fruit trees had plenty of blossom. The walnut tree which grew at the end of the garden, by the Baileys' wall, was in young auburn leaf.

Everything, Harold thought, looked in good heart, and when Phil came from the house to join him, he thought how well she looked too. There was a radiance about her which was new.

Of course, he told himself, he had never known the girl

when she had been free of worry. Now, with the winter and its tragedy behind her, she seemed to be responding to the spring with all the natural joy of young things. How easy it would be to take the plunge, to ask her to marry him, to leave it to the gods – and to Phil – to arrange his future!

He realized that she was looking at him, as though she read his thoughts.

She put out a hand and touched his arm, speaking quickly as though she had just come to a decision.

'Come and sit down for a minute. I've something to tell you.'

He followed her to an old garden seat which the admiral had placed years ago in a sunny corner against a southern wall. At Harold's feet an early bee was rolling over and over, its striped furry body entwined with a wallflower blossom from which it was zealously extracting the honey.

'I've some wonderful news,' said Phil, 'and I want you to be the first to know. Can you guess?'

Harold looked at her. He had always thought that poets grossly overstated things when they talked of eyes like stars. Now he began to understand.

'I was never good at guessing,' he confessed.

'I only knew myself yesterday. Frank has asked me to marry him. Say you're pleased.'

Harold took a deep breath. If he felt a pang of jealousy, it vanished at once. Wholeheartedly, he congratulated her.

'He's the luckiest devil in the world,' he told her sincerely, taking her hands in his.

'He's coming here tomorrow to arrange things with the rector,' said Phil. 'We had the longest telephone talk ever known to the Lulling exchange last night. We shall get married this summer.'

She leant forward and kissed Harold on the cheek.

'And will you give me away?' she asked.

'It's like asking me to part with my heart,' replied Harold, half-meaning it, 'but since you ask me, I shall count it an honour, my dear.'

They stood up and gazed across the garden.

'Will you leave Thrush Green?' asked Harold.

'We haven't got that far,' smiled Phil. 'But I don't think I could ever leave Tullivers. We could build on, I suppose.'

She looked about her vaguely, trying to envisage the future, and suddenly became conscious of the wonder of a life which contained such a precious element as sure joy to come.

She turned to Harold wonderingly.

'What is it about Thrush Green which makes it so special? Is it the air, or the green, or the people?'

Harold considered the question seriously before he spoke. In the silence between them they could hear the distant sounds of a Thrush Green morning. Miss Fogerty's children called to each other in the playground, the rooks cawed above St Andrew's elms, and Winnie Bailey's voice could be heard as she opened a window to the sunshine.

'All those things make Thrush Green,' said Harold, 'and much, much more.'

He thought of his own restless wanderings abroad, and his present joy. Here he had found a home and deep happiness. He knew he shared this feeling with the girl beside him. Thrush Green seemed to have some magic quality which they both recognized instinctively.

'The power of healing,' said Harold softly, as if to himself.